DAUGHTER *of* POMPEII

Lorraine Blundell

authorHOUSE

AuthorHouse™ UK
1663 Liberty Drive
Bloomington, IN 47403 USA
www.authorhouse.co.uk
Phone: 0800.197.4150

© 2019 Lorraine Blundell. All rights reserved.

No part of this book may be reproduced, stored in a retrieval system, or transmitted by any means without the written permission of the author.

Published by AuthorHouse 05/14/2019

ISBN: 978-1-7283-8787-1 (sc)
ISBN: 978-1-7283-8788-8 (e)

Print information available on the last page.

Any people depicted in stock imagery provided by Getty Images are models, and such images are being used for illustrative purposes only.
Certain stock imagery © Getty Images.

This book is printed on acid-free paper.

Because of the dynamic nature of the Internet, any web addresses or links contained in this book may have changed since publication and may no longer be valid. The views expressed in this work are solely those of the author and do not necessarily reflect the views of the publisher, and the publisher hereby disclaims any responsibility for them.

For Jenni and Steve

'The area around Pompeii was famous for its perfume made from roses. Roses were often painted or carved on ceilings and were associated with secrecy. Hence, the expression *sub rosa*.'

Karen's Garden Tips 2015

Author's Note

To avoid confusion the novel's main character is referred to as Poppy. Her historical name was Poppaea Sabina (the Younger).
Her mother was Poppaea Sabina (the Elder).

CHARACTERS

Claudius Caesar	Emperor of Rome
Messalina	Empress of Rome
Nero Claudius Caesar	Emperor of Rome
Agrippina	His mother
Octavia	Empress of Rome
Claudia Acte	Nero's mistress
Seneca	Nero's tutor
Sporus	Imperial freedman
Neophytus	Imperial freedman
Epaphroditos	Imperial freedman

Poppaea (the Younger) (Poppy)	Empress of Rome
Poppaea (the Elder)	Her mother
Lentullus Scipio	Her step brother
Valerius Asiaticus	Roman Consul & Senator
Helius	Court Administrator
Farzana	Poppy's best friend *
Aeneus Capito	Her husband, Praetorian
Aulus	Her father *
Marcellus	Her brother *
Aeliana	His wife *
Rufrius Crispinus Poppy's first husband	Praetorian Prefect
Rufrius Crispinus	Their son
Tigellinus	Praetorian Prefect
Marcus	His second in command *
Galba	Roman general
Salvius Otho Poppy's second husband	Friend of Nero
Locusta	Notorious Roman poisoner

Clodius Flaccus	Duumvir of Pompeii
Prima	Elite courtesan
Sempronius Verus	Owner, Gentlemen's Club
Lucius Diomedes	Senator for Pompeii
Caecilius Jucundus	Wealthy banker
Julia Felix	Property owner
Cleandros	Her business manager *
Cornelius Sulpicius	Inn owner
Umbricius Scaurus	Garum exporter
Celer & Severus	Nero's architects
Aelianus	Chariot racing trainer *
Varus	Thief *
Vibius	Scribe*
Livia	Owner, cosmetics shop *
Drusilla	Owner, perfume shop *
Drusis	Cook, Gentlemen's Club *
Hinnulus	Fresco painter *
Valentius	Commander, Nuceria

* Denotes non historical character

Prologue

ROME

The Palatine Hill

47 A.D.

An ancient, derelict hovel hugged the slopes of the Palatine Hill. It was tiny and so hidden by the overgrowth surrounding it, that an interloper could come upon it before becoming aware of its existence. The woman inside sat engrossed in a task in which she was obviously experienced. The beginning of a humpback was evidence enough that her youth was behind her. She was tall and thin and her matted hair streaked with grey hung down past her shoulders.

As she worked, Locusta muttered to herself.

Her head jerked upwards as she heard a footfall outside the door, and she shrank back against the wall. A woman covered in black, her face hidden by a hood, entered and gazed around her.

'I'm told your name is Locusta,' she uttered softly.

'Who wants to know?'

'My name is Poppaea.'

'Ah! Let me look at you.' Locusta moved forward more quickly than her visitor would have imagined her capable. With a jerk she pulled away Poppaea's hood. 'Yes, you're as beautiful as they say you are,' she said thoughtfully as she gazed at her visitor. 'I'm not surprised to see you,' she continued, her voice low and raspy. 'You're in a bit of trouble, aren't you!'

Surprised by the woman's words, Poppaea looked around her. The hut was circular with lit candles ringing most of the interior. Nonetheless, it was dim inside. There was a simple, earthen floor. Poppaea's gaze was drawn towards the plants that were massed haphazardly on a couple of benchtops and on the counter where Locusta had been working with a pestle and mortarium. The hovel had a stink all its own although it stood hidden very close to the luxury palaces of the Emperor and the ultra-wealthy of Rome.

'There is nowhere else to turn,' Poppaea told the poisoner. 'Others have caused my downfall. Now, to save my daughter's reputation I must take the honourable way out.'

The older woman sighed. 'Always that seems to be the case. Honour! What is it really worth?' She paused as she studied Poppaea. 'So, you've come to me seeking a poison that will give you a quick death?'

'Yes.' It occurred to her that this old woman would be unlikely to know the meaning of the word *honour*.

'You're not the first, nor will you be the last,' Locusta whispered. 'A wealthy woman whose name I daren't utter has just been here seeking the future death of her husband. It is too soon for her to act yet but when the time comes, I will do as she asks and in return, she'll have no choice but to pay me exactly what I demand. What is the worth of a human life do you think?' She gave a ghastly smile. 'I tell you only because you are powerless, as you seek nothing more from life. Already, your spirit begins to fade.

Do you know there are many flowers so beautiful that they would take your breath away, but they hold death within them? You shake your head, so I will tell you that the blue flowers that hide aconite or the deceptive, cloying sweetness of pink oleander blossoms are only two of many. Sit. I'll make the draught now.' She pointed to the only seat in the hut. 'The cost will be ten gold aurei.'

Poppaea nodded. As the poisoner worked, she sat silently watching. Numb with grief, she tried valiantly to reconcile herself to her fate.

When the potion was ready and the money had been paid, Poppaea pulled her hood up over her face once more and crept out into the darkness. A quick glance reassured her that she appeared to be alone. Then she drifted like a wraith in the night towards her carriage.

After she'd gone, Locusta counted the coins again then added them to a filthy old bag hidden under a mound of dirt. She'd soon have enough to buy a respectable home, probably not on the Palatine, but in a good area of Rome. Perhaps, she might also own the school she'd always dreamed of where students would pay her to learn her craft.

Death was going to make her a very wealthy woman.

Part I

44 A.D.

In the Beginning

1

POMPEII

The forum

It was early morning. Nonetheless, the heat was already oppressive. The pale blue sky overhead seemed to have been swept clean of any hint of clouds by some unseen hand, and even the sound of water spilling from fountains in the gardens of the wealthy gave little relief. A sense of heavy listlessness settled over the city.

As was usual in Roman cities, the forum was the focus of activities in Pompeii. People met there to gossip, discuss the latest news and argue over politics. They attended the nearby bathhouse and temples and conducted civil matters in the Basilica.

Food kiosks catered especially for those who had enough money to buy cuts of meat and the freshest fish. There were also surprising varieties of other offerings available for purchase. These ranged from lamps and sandals to jewellery trinkets and many more. It was even possible to buy slaves who were transported to Pompeii from all corners of the Empire.

A girl stood alone in front of buckets of flowers, her arms filled with blossoms, their colours as vibrant as a rainbow. Around her passed a chattering, sweating crowd of people all intent on their various personal pursuits. It was not yet the busiest time of the day in the middle of summer.

A short distance away a girl of about her own age approached with an older woman clutching a bag. As they drew closer the flower seller heard their conversation.

'Come along Poppy, we haven't got all day!' Amira, her mother's favourite slave, frowned at the girl dawdling beside her. 'We must get this chicken back to the house in plenty of time for cook to prepare dinner.'

'But we only just got here!' Poppy complained.

Amira shook her head and sighed as she wiped the sweat off her forehead with her hand. She disliked food shopping trips to the forum especially with Poppy, but cook had excused herself from her usual task, on the basis of a heavy load of cooking, as visitors were expected for dinner.

The flower seller, Farzana, smiled at the other girl as she walked closer looking sullen and unhappy. 'Here!' Impulsively, Farzana thrust a red rose towards her. 'This is for you.'

Poppy stared at her then pausing, took the flower. 'What's your name?' she asked.

'Farzana.'

'I'm Poppy,' she stated with a small smile.

Then she was gone pulled along by Amira, pushing through the gathering wall of people around them, as the level of noise increased minute by minute. Leaving the forum they entered Via Stabiana and hurried towards home.

Villa Poppaeus on Vicolo del Menandro proclaimed the wealth of the family who owned it. It was well located in one of the best areas of the city and took up most of the large block on which it stood. An understated front entry led into an impressive atrium, huge in size and decorated with gloriously coloured wall frescoes. The owner's wealth had been created over the years with profits earned from a highly successful tile factory.

Curious passers-by craned their necks in an attempt to sneak a peek at the luxury that lay within, but the family guarded their privacy well, and little could be seen without entering. While they waited for an audience a few of the public were privileged to claim a place to sit on the stone bench that stood beside the front entry.

It was to this distinctive villa that Poppy walked with Amira. She was surprised when they arrived to see her mother pacing the floor waiting for them.

'Finally, there you are! What took you so long?'

Amira glanced accusingly at Poppy. 'The forum was very crowded today, Domina,' she replied bluntly.

'Why is it important?' Poppy asked curiously.

'We have a special visitor waiting to meet you,' Poppy's mother said as she cast her eyes over her wayward daughter. 'Tidy yourself then come through to the garden.'

Leaving the spacious atrium Poppy's mother, Poppaea, quickly made her way into the pretty peristyle garden. Waiting for her was her step-son, Lentulus Scipio, and a stern-faced, older man of unremarkable appearance who appeared to be intently studying a graceful statue of Venus. Unknown to anyone else, he was trying to decide whether the goddess was modestly trying to cover her intimate parts with her hands, or perhaps seductively drawing attention to her femininity. He turned towards Poppaea as she arrived.

'Your daughter is here now?'

'Yes, Rufrius. I'm so sorry to have kept you waiting, you arrived a little earlier than expected.'

'It's no matter,' he answered diplomatically. 'If your daughter has inherited your beauty the wait will have been worth it.' When Poppy finally hurried through the colonnade he found that he couldn't take his eyes off her. She was a beautiful younger version of her mother, famous for her looks.

Lentulus rose to leave. 'I'll see you back in Rome,' he grinned at Rufrius, 'I'm sure you can handle today's business without me.'

Rufrius nodded without taking his gaze off the girl. She was tall with long auburn hair swept back from a face with skin like alabaster. When she looked up at him he saw that her eyes were the colour of the sea.

Poppaea turned to her daughter. 'Poppy, this is Rufrius Crispinus, Prefect of the praetorian guard of the Emperor Claudius,' she told her. 'He's visiting us this morning. Here, sit down with me,' Poppaea gestured towards the space beside her as she spoke.

'Well, Poppy, I'm glad to have the pleasure of meeting you. Have you ever been to Rome?' Rufrius asked when she was seated and he was able to really study her more closely. She was very young, he thought, but that shouldn't be an impediment to marriage between them. He'd also wait a little after the betrothal. What really impressed him, was that he'd seen many women in his time, but this girl was lovely beyond compare.

'I've been there on several occasions when I was younger, sir,' she replied to his question.

'Would you enjoy living in Rome do you think?' Rufrius asked casually, but the question was of major importance. Beauty aside, he had no intention of undertaking marriage to a girl who was antagonistic to the very idea of residing in Rome.

Poppy smiled broadly and her whole face lit up. 'I'd love to live there. I've heard that it's so much more exciting than Pompeii.'

Rufrius looked over at Poppaea and nodded that he'd made his decision. As he rose to go he smiled kindly at Poppy. 'Then

Daughter of Pompeii

I believe I can make your dream come true. Salve, Poppy, I'm so very glad to have met you.'

She remained sitting in the garden as her mother walked with their visitor to the villa's front door where they stopped for a few moments to speak.

'If you're happy with the marriage, then I'll leave the betrothal arrangements to you,' Rufrius informed her crisply. 'You have a very beautiful daughter. I trust you'll chaperone her appropriately until she becomes my wife.'

'Of course. There's no need to concern yourself on that matter,' Poppaea assured him. 'She's led a sheltered life and always been chaperoned as she should have been. We are a highly respected family here in Pompeii.'

They parted with the decision concluded to the satisfaction of both. Poppaea, however, did not miss the hint of a warning in his tone.

Rufrius left the villa with a spring in his step. He slid his hand over his black, slicked back hair and smiled. He was of Egyptian birth with swarthy skin and had come to Rome as a fish merchant. He vowed that he'd have his revenge for the insults and sneers he'd endured at the hands of some of Rome's aristocracy. He'd become a praetorian guard and advanced up the chain of command until he became praetorian prefect.

Now he'd take the next step, this time on the social ladder. Not only would he marry a beautiful woman, but one who belonged to the patrician class, even if only a minor one from Pompeii.

He walked aimlessly, lost in thought until he found himself close to the Venus district of the city, judging by the increasing number of street prostitutes. Pompeii's district of love was always popular. Rufrius stopped at a street food bar where he purchased a cup of wine.

'Friend,' he smiled at the man who served him, 'where can I find the city's most skilled lady of love to keep me company?' He winked.

'That would be Prima,' the slave grinned. 'She lives only a couple of streets from here, further away from this district, but maybe you can't afford her. It'll cost you plenty!' He stretched out his arm and indicated the direction Rufrius should take. 'Ask again at the Gentlemen's Club! It may be that she's working there today.'

2

The Gentlemen's Club
(House of the Centenary)

Via di Nola

Prima held her hands over her ears and grimaced as the club's owner, Sempronius Verus, barely avoided being hit by a flying amphora flung at his head by the club's temperamental cook, Drusus.

'Get out and stay out!' he roared furiously.

'Go hang yourself!' Drusus shouted at him as he ran past Prima and out into the street.

'What brought that on?' she asked as calm returned, at least temporarily.

'I refused to pay him more money. He's not worth it. Now, of course, I've got the problem of replacing him before dinner tonight. Sometimes I think this club's just too much trouble,' Sempronius grumbled.

Prima smiled. She knew that the club was undoubtedly worth a fortune in gold. Sempronius made money from the richest men in Pompeii. They paid handsomely for the privilege of membership in this exclusive retreat away from the noise and lower classes of the city, not to mention the nagging of their wives.

There was no question that Prima was by far the most beautiful and elite courtesan in Pompeii or Herculaneum.

'Do you have a booking this morning Prima?' Sempronius asked in a calmer voice. 'Perhaps you'd like something to drink first?'

In more private moments, he acknowledged to himself that if he thought about it, he was actually at least a little in love with her. Her voice was like silk and her laugh, like liquid silver.

'I have a few minutes before my gentleman arrives,' she said. 'I'll have one of your lemon ices if I may.' The two had grown to know each other quite well over the three years since her arrival. She paid him a small percentage of her earnings when working at the club to cover the use of a cubicle. She always requested the only one that included a private bathing area, as was appropriate to the status of her customers.

Sempronius liked to watch her as she sat waiting, her stunning beauty adding to the visual delights that he already provided. She was also a profitable business asset.

His thoughts were rudely interrupted by one of the kitchen staff: 'The water's busted again!' the kitchen maid, Aya whined. 'How am I supposed to clean the bowls?'

Excusing himself with a distracted smile at Prima, Sempronius fled towards the kitchen. This day seemed to be quickly descending into chaos.

The services offered by the gentlemen's club were many and varied and it was the only one of its kind in the city.

As it was lavishly appointed and strictly discrete about its members' activities, personal or otherwise, there was always a long waiting list. The club was situated in a quiet location not too much of a walk from the forum.

On more than one occasion, Sempronius had been guilty of peeping through a spy hole in one of the cubiculum walls while Prima entertained a client. He envied them their pleasure. Afterwards, he'd slunk away feeling guilty and hoping that no one had seen him.

Originally a very large residential villa with a lovely peristyle, set within an extensive sunken garden, the club's furnishings were exquisite and expensive. Colourful classically themed frescoes adorned the walls and intricate mosaics decorated the floors. The perfume from precious imported cedarwood tables, reminiscent of the east, complimented the fragrance wafting from vases of freshly cut flowers, and silky soft cushions sat plumped up ready to relax weary backs.

From a nymphaeum towards the rear of the triclinium, in the villa's garden, the relaxing sound of running water could be heard as it tumbled over a high niche into a clear pool below and outside, amidst the cypress pines, strutted an arrogant, brilliantly coloured peacock.

To ensure security, two large, uniformed slaves guarded the outer door. Inside, were several large rooms where comfort was guaranteed, as well as service by well-trained slaves gliding so silently as to seem almost magical.

Highly confidential business meetings were held in formal rooms available for that purpose without the risk of proceedings being overheard by rivals, and messengers were kept busy at such times arranging the services of local scribes who arrived at the club as required.

There was no doubt, however, that the club's most popular attraction was the service of procuring young women. They were carefully selected by Sempronius himself. Prima had wondered from time to time how much in-depth he made the process.

The girls came unobtrusively at the required time, arriving one by one, to provide personal services to those gentlemen who wished to pay for pleasure in cubicles containing comfortable beds. Located down a long hallway with views to the secluded private gardens at the back of the villa, these rooms were rarely empty and brought in massive profits to the club.

The villa was vast and unquestionably a place of ultimate privilege and privacy, and its members obsessively guarded all knowledge of what went on within its walls. A list of members' names was not available no matter who requested it.

'Here is your flavoured ice, lady,' a slave bowed gracefully as she placed the elegant, glass dish on the side table. 'Is there anything more that I can bring you?'

Casually slipping a coin to her, Prima murmured 'That will be all for now.' The dessert was cooling, with just a touch of tartness in its taste.

It was here, in this setting of luxury and secrecy, that Prima sat waiting for her client. As she did so, she considered the events of the previous year. She was well on the way to becoming wealthy. Prima owned a small but comfortable house in Pompeii. It had taken all of her savings but she knew that it was worth it to ensure she'd always have a roof over her head. She never conducted "business" there.

When she'd finished with her client she intended to stroll sedately home. She changed her mind, however, when she was propositioned just before leaving by a tall stranger from Rome who introduced himself as Rufrius.

He left after a lengthy session, very pleased with his time with Prima. He'd needed it to blunt his thoughts of the pleasure to come after he'd married the beautiful Poppy. The day had turned out well.

Daughter of Pompeii

As mid-afternoon arrived Farzana watched as her older brother, Marcellus, wheeled their creaky, old handcart to the edge of the forum. It was a place reserved for pedestrian use only. Occasionally, vendors complained at having to carry their stock from the street, but on the whole, the rule was popular.

Flower sales had kept Farzana busy and she had little remaining of her stock. She decided to return for a while in the afternoon after lunch when she'd collected more flowers to sell.

'It's been a good morning, I see,' Marcellus grinned. 'Father will be pleased. We can certainly use the extra money. It mightn't be much but you do a good job and it all helps. Let's go home.'

Farzana and Marcellus lived with their elderly father in a small house in Via Consolare. The street was near the forum and they chatted happily until they arrived.

Their father, Aulus, was busy working, as usual, on repairs to customers' sandals. Pompeii's citizens brought their shoes to him usually in expectation that by some miracle, he could repair their worn footwear so that it looked like it was new. Now and again, but not often enough, someone would actually buy new sandals that he'd made from the softest leather. Such sales achieved the best profit.

The tiny room at the front served as the shop. It was Marcellus who travelled around sourcing the leather Aulus used, and also the supplies of flowers grown in the Campania region that were sold by Farzana. He bought the best quality of both for the cheapest available prices.

Their home was clean and tidy and stood near the Herculaneum Gate. At the back of the house was a garden adjacent to the city wall. It was small but there were two olive trees with silvery leaves that stood beside a graceful bird bath. Farzana liked to sit on the bench there watching the birds as they frolicked and dipped their wings into the water, causing silvery baubles to fly into the air. They sparkled in the Pompeii sunlight.

They were a family who bothered no one and lived a quiet life except for attending the annual musical festival at the great theatre, or an occasional outing to the arena to watch the gladiators fight. Marcellus had lately become attracted to a local girl called Aeliana, but Farzana seemed to be happy simply spending time at home with their father when she wasn't working.

She loved the smell of the leather as he moulded it skilfully into soft, luxury sandals. She seemed unaware of her own dark, striking good looks and the glances that followed her petite figure wherever she went.

As daylight began to fade, she sat alone enjoying the garden's peace as the noise of the city died away and the heat of the day lessened. Today had been interesting, she thought. Most of all, she knew that one day she'd like very much to meet Poppy again.

3

Poppy sat in her room when Rufrius had gone, wondering if she'd misunderstood what had just happened. Had he asked for her in marriage? Her gaze went to the pretty pink oleanders blooming outside her window.

'Come in,' she responded to a soft knock at the door she recognised as her mother's usual request for entry.

'Did you like him?' Poppaea asked with a tinge of excitement in her voice.

'I suppose so.'

'That's good,' Poppaea smiled.

'Why?'

Her mother reached over to touch her cheek. 'You do know that you're of an age to be married, Poppy, don't you?'

'Couldn't it wait until I'm older though?' she suggested hopefully.

'Rufrius has asked to become betrothed to you but he won't wait forever. With your poor father dead we are reliant on your stepfather, and you know how "careful" he is with money. Come, smile for me!'

Poppy managed a somewhat uncertain smile.

'We'll talk again in more detail when the marriage is closer.' Poppaea stood up to leave.

'I'd like to go for a walk on my own for a while,' Poppy suggested.

'Don't be too long,' Poppaea warned before leaving the room, 'and don't talk to anyone you don't know.'

Poppy stepped out into the sunshine deciding which way to walk. She rather liked the hustle and bustle of the forum so decided to go there. She'd take her time inspecting what was for sale at the various stalls. The warmth of the sun lifted her mood. Perhaps she should spend a few minutes first, to pray for the success of her coming marriage. With that in mind, she turned her steps towards the synagogue.

The Jewish synagogue was located in a quiet side street. It was well kept and catered to the needs of Pompeii's small Jewish population. Both Poppy and her mother were Jewish and belonged to the synagogue which had as its congregation rich, poor and those in-between.

Poppy entered the quiet, dim prayer hall through the women's entrance. She sat in peace for some time in the semi darkness and when she left after seeking guidance, she felt more at peace.

Humming to herself she walked along the narrow footpath and entered the forum. By now, it was the middle of the afternoon but some shoppers still remained there. Most of the others were attending the baths, temples or Basilica, bathing being the most popular.

She saw Farzana standing where Poppy had last seen her. She had just sold a bunch of flowers to a customer and he paid her. She looked up and smiled as she saw Poppy approaching.

Daughter of Pompeii

'Are you feeling happier now?' Farzana asked as she placed the coins from the sale into her purse.

'Yes. I'm to be married,' Poppy blurted out. 'Will you be finished here shortly?' As soon as she'd spoken, she wondered why she was telling such important news to a complete stranger, but there was something about the flower girl that was sweet and invited confidence.

Farzana glanced up at the sun dial. 'In just a few minutes actually.' She gestured towards Marcellus who was walking towards them. 'Would you like to sit in the gardens at the Temple of Venus and maybe we could talk for a while?'

Poppy nodded. As Marcellus packed up the flower buckets they left and soon found a seat outside the temple, which was close to the forum.

As they talked, the two young women became oblivious to those passing by through the Marine Gate. Even the beauty of where they were and the sombre and prayerful attitude of visitors to the temple didn't distract them. It wasn't until the sun began to set that they realised how long they'd been sitting there.

'Let's do this again,' Poppy laughed.

'I'd love to,' Farzana agreed.

And so began a friendship that was to remain through the turbulent years ahead. Neither one of them could have imagined the pain or the joy that was lying in wait for them.

The summer passed quickly and the cool breezes of autumn began to give notice of an approaching winter. No doubt the braziers would be needed to provide heating for the cold. Rufrius found that he could wait no longer and soon became betrothed to Poppy. On the third finger of her left hand he placed the Truth Ring of betrothal.

There were several furniture shops in Pompeii that had amongst their stock various marriage chests. Poppaea urgently visited all of them to buy the best available. The last of the shops, in Via Stabiana, had exactly what she was looking for. She entered and when the owner had finished with the current customer, he approached her.

'Lady, what can I provide for you?' he enquired politely.

'Show me your best marriage chest!' Poppaea demanded.

'It's very beautiful. I'm sure you'll like it,' he told her as he led her towards the back of the shop and removed a coverlet covering the chest.

Poppaea clapped her hands with excitement. 'It's stunning!' Without even asking the price, she decided then and there to buy it for her daughter.

Made of wood with an aromatic fragrance, the chest looked antique. It was large and decorated with golden figures of the gods and acanthus leaves. Poppaea knew she had excelled herself.

Slaves carried it back to the villa. When Poppy saw it she threw her arms around her mother.

'Thank you. Thank you. I'll never forget this moment.'

From that day on it seemed that the hours were filled with sewing and visits to various fabric shops. Poppaea had excellent taste and chose the most beautiful garments and other items she could afford. Many of the fabrics were silk in a variety of colours. One was a pale green that heightened the beauty of Poppy's auburn hair and green eyes.

'Mother, can we go to Farzana's house and look at the new sandals her father makes?' Poppy pleaded one morning. 'I've heard people say that he's the best sandal-maker in the city.'

Her mother smiled indulgently and together they walked to the house of Aulus. Farzana saw them coming and ran to welcome them. 'It's so wonderful that you've come. Please step inside and meet my father.'

After the introductions were finished Poppy flitted from one pair of sandals to the other overcome with excitement. Finally, she chose two pairs made from luxurious leather and ornamented with pretty gemstones.

Poppaea had scrimped and saved, even taking money from her household budget so that she could provide the highest quality of everything for her daughter. She was determined that Poppy would begin her new life in the best possible way. The purchase of the sandals was only one of many in the months following her daughter's betrothal.

After their visitors had gone, Aulus turned to Farzana. 'You have a lovely friend,' he remarked, 'and she's certainly beautiful.' Then his expression turned into a slight frown. 'It's strange. I can't quite tell you why, but there's something about her that sends a warning. Maybe, I'm just getting old.' He shook his head and went back to working on the repair job that he'd been doing before Poppaea and Poppy's arrival.

His words were soon forgotten by both himself and Farzana as the days and months passed. But they would eventually come back to haunt him.

4

Dark clouds settled over the city of Pompeii on the day Poppy wed Rufrius Crispinus. Rain pelted down swept sideways by the wind onto the roads' thick basalt slabs heavily rutted by the wheels of carts and carriages. The stiff breeze made matters worse for those attempting to cross the streets over thick stepping stones from one footpath to the other. Life was a misery for anyone foolishly trying to transport goods from one part of Pompeii to another and on the harbour, the waves were whipped into a frenzy as they slapped against the pier, resulting in the taxation kiosk being closed for the day.

Vesuvius loomed over all, its peak shrouded in mist and the vineyards that clung to its sides dripped with the constant rain. Many of Pompeii's residents remained indoors.

The villa of Poppy's family, however, looked at its very best, scrubbed and cleaned until everything shone and the fragrance of roses hung in the air. A group of witnesses had been invited, and Rufrius was attended by friends looking resplendent in the full ceremonial uniform of the praetorian guard. Neighbours and friends of the family also came to watch and wish Poppy luck.

It was said later that every man who saw the bride wished that he was Rufrius that day. Poppy wore a traditional long white robe, the tunica reata, with a woollen belt tied in a knot of Hercules. She'd been dressed by her mother, as required by tradition. Her long, auburn hair fell in loose waves down her back, covered by a flame coloured veil.

It was a formal ceremony and Poppy gave her vow in a soft but firm voice amidst total silence.

Quando tu Gaius, ego Gaia.

Farzana had been invited and stood watching with Marcellus. She was happy for her friend but sad that she'd no longer see her. Poppy had earlier reassured her that she'd be sure to visit Pompeii from time to time but Farzana wasn't convinced.

Poppy felt a mixture of excitement and fear of the unknown. Her mother had briefly prepared her for what was to follow but she trembled with apprehension that night as Rufrius untied the knotted belt around her waist.

'You're shaking, Poppy,' Rufrius said softly as he held her to him gently and kissed her. 'Trust me. I'll hurt you as little as possible. It will be quick and then everything will become easier.' Having removed her robe, he laid her down on the wedding bed. What followed was a shock, and she found the experience unpleasant and invasive despite her new husband's kind words, but Rufrius was an experienced lover and he calmed her fear.

The next morning, they were seen off by a small crowd and she heard Farzana's voice calling, 'Poppy, I'll miss you!' as the carriage left them behind. The newly married couple left Pompeii for Rome and a new life stretched before her.

Farzana turned to leave and looked across at Poppaea who was trying to wipe away her tears, but in vain. 'Leave without me, I'll be home soon,' she whispered to Marcellus.

Then she went to Poppaea's side and spoke gently to her. 'Your daughter is the most beautiful bride I've ever seen. She looks more like a goddess. You've done such a wonderful job. You must be proud.'

Poppaea's tears overflowed down her cheeks. She had no idea what she would do without the daughter she loved so deeply.

'I know I'm not Poppy, but I'll be here for you,' Farzana reassured her. 'It's time you looked after yourself. You deserve something special after all you've done. Why don't we take a walk down to the perfume shop on Via di Castricio. There's nothing like perfume to lift our spirits and perhaps you'll smell something you like.'

Later that day, after Farzana had left her following the visit to the perfume shop Poppaea thought about her kindness. She was a loving, gentle person, and Poppy was fortunate to have her for a friend.

Farzana and Poppaea fell into the habit of meeting occasionally for a chat over a cool drink, and became firm friends. Poppy was not to return to Pompeii for some time.

As they approached Rome, Poppy gazed out the window of the carriage at the grim gravestones and mausoleums that lined the Via Appia. Some of them looked very old. It reminded her a little of the Via delle Tombe outside Pompeii's Herculaneum Gate. But this road was crowded with a variety of travellers and led to the city of Rome. A sense of excitement replaced her trepidation as they entered through the city's massive walls.

Travelling along narrow, unnamed streets busy with people all going about their business, they passed near the fringe of the Forum and the Circus Maximus, then began the steep ascent up the Aventine Hill.

'I hope you won't be too disappointed,' Rufrius told her as the carriage stopped outside a small but neat house on the side of the hill. 'I'm not a wealthy man, at least not yet.'

Poppy stared at the house intently. It was pretty, she decided. The garden was manicured and the steps freshly painted. She turned to Rufrius, 'I'm sure this looks just perfect.'

Inside, the house had a sleeping cubiculum of moderate size, a second one much smaller, a small triclinium that was long and narrow and a tiny storage area. A kitchen was nearby, outside. At the rear, there was a small garden with lemon trees.

Poppy wandered through the house noting the absence of any type of atrium. She was disappointed as she'd have preferred to have one. Then, she made her way through to the garden. The day was sunny with a slight breeze as she sat down. Rufrius walked slowly up to join her.

'I'm so sorry this isn't quite what you're used to,' her told her with a look of embarrassment. 'Hopefully, it won't be long before I get more pay and we can move to somewhere more appropriate.'

Poppy reached up and took his hand. 'I like it here. The house has charm and I'll plant more flowers in the garden to make it even better.'

Rufrius bent down, took her hand and kissed it.

It was perhaps at this moment that he began to truly love Poppy. He had coveted her for her beauty, but before long he found himself obsessively in love with her. Their days were peaceful and contented for a few years and it seemed that this was a marriage that was a success. Poppy was happy.

Lorraine Blundell

The Gardens of Lucullus

Valerius Asiaticus looked out of the library window at the view of the stunning gardens of Lucullus that he'd purchased so recently when he'd become consul for the second time. On a day like this with a gentle, sweet breeze and the sun glinting on the water gushing from a central fountain, in itself a work of creative genius, this was paradise. The gardens were ancient but had survived the continuing acquisition of such estates for development in the expanding city, not to mention the avarice of a passing parade of emperors. The view of Rome below the gardens was arguably the best in the city.

He wondered how everything had gone so wrong.

He considered Claudius an old fool, emperor or not. He'd relinquished his power to Messalina, that liar of a woman he'd married. Asiaticus had been shocked to learn of rumours that he himself stood accused of treason for attempting to raise a force against Rome and for adultery. He pondered where ludicrous accusations like these came from. He suspected that Messalina coveted his possessions, especially the gardens.

Valerius had twice been consul of Rome. Any fool would realise that a man like that with a good reputation, which he certainly had, would be the most unlikely suspect in such a situation. Rome had become corrupt and run by people with too much power who sought even more.

And what of Poppaea?

Valerius was most disturbed by the mention of her name in relation to these accusations. Yes, they were friends, but nothing more. She was kind and loyal. The only reason that occurred to him was that Messalina had done this out of spite.

Even though Valerius knew that the accusations were untrue, even he was powerless to refute them in the face of the treachery of Messalina and her aide, Lucius Vitellius, a man with a twisted, corrupt outlook on life, who clung onto her like a leech.

Valerius took the only course of action left to him. He left Rome for a trip to the luxury holiday centre of Baiae, hoping that in his absence the rumours would die down.

The Royal Palace
The Palatine

The royal palace was a hotbed of intrigue. Messalina sat whispering with Vitellius. 'They were lovers, I'm sure of it,' Messalina declared with certainty. 'Poppaea has planned this with him. They're both guilty of treason! She can't be allowed to escape her punishment. With any luck, she'll lose that lovely head of hers!'

As usual, Vitellius agreed with her outburst, while at the same time fearing a day would come when he could expect to join those who had annoyed the Empress. He knew when that happened, he would pay the usual price.

Vitellius shivered.

Together they confronted Claudius. Giving little consideration to the accusations, which were manufactured and contained nothing of substance, he panicked, expecting to see a rebellion in the city streets at any minute, and pronounced his belief in their assertions.

Claudius made no allowance for a fair hearing for Asiaticus before the senate, ordering that he be captured immediately and brought back. This was not accepted practice for a Roman citizen of such distinction.

It was Rufrius Crispinus, commander of the Guard who was sent with troops to return Valerius Asiaticus in chains to Rome. He was uncomfortable with hunting down a man who'd given such eminent service to Rome, but he had no option. The least he could do, though, he told himself as he and his praetorians rode swiftly on their mission, was to show every respect and consideration for the man he was seeking.

They found him in Baiae.

'Do not enter the estate,' Rufrius ordered the troopers, 'until I tell you to do so.' Then, he went in search of Valerius. He found him sitting alone at the back of his villa, quietly gazing out across the bay.

Rufrius looked around and saw that no one else was present. They were totally alone.

'Sir,' he addressed Asiaticus, 'I see you are enjoying the peace here. It is, indeed a beautiful place!'

Valerius acknowledged him with a wave of his hand to join him. 'Please sit.'

'I regret that isn't possible,' Rufrius said softly. 'I have no choice, against my personal wish, but to arrest you by order of the Emperor. The charge is treason and adultery. I take no joy in this, you have my personal apology. Sir, will you please stand.'

Valerius stood.

'Thank you, commander,' he replied, as he looked directly into Rufrius' eyes. 'I see that you are a man of honour.'

Rufrius walked with Valerius towards the waiting praetorians, chained him, then took him back to Rome. He'd carried out his orders. Shortly after he returned to the city, he was awarded one and a half million sestertii by a grateful senate and given the title of praetor. But it brought him little joy, even though this would be enough, financially, to enable him to meet the rules to enter the senate. He would have no difficulty meeting the financial requirement.

The Royal Palace

'You know this accusation is false!' Valerius Asiaticus stood before Claudius pleading his case in a small room of the palace.

He was still in chains, a degrading experience for a man of his reputation. Messalina sat in a corner remaining very still. She was also silent.

The damage she'd inflicted was already done.

'I've given my life to Rome's defence. Surely you can see that my enemies are seeking to destroy me. At least let me defend myself before the senate,' Asiaticus pleaded. He was well aware that senators would restore his freedom with a 'not guilty' finding by a huge margin. It was his final hope.

Claudius began to waver a little. Messalina glared at him.

He cleared his throat and gave his verdict. 'It's true that you've been a staunch supporter of Rome in the past,' he answered, as Messalina glared at him, 'but I can't take the risk of leaving you alive. It's unthinkable that we could have rebellion in our streets. However, because of your past service, I give you the choice as to how you wish to die. I release you to your villa. In three days if you are still alive when the guards arrive, they will carry out your execution. Goodbye, Asiaticus. You may leave.'

There was a tight, smug smile on Messalina's face.

Valerius returned to his villa and gardens. He struggled on that first day to accept the injustice of Claudius' decision. As a military man, he could tolerate just about anything except weakness. How, he wondered, had the great Roman Empire ended up with an emperor like this one?

He rejected the idea that Claudius didn't understand what his decision really meant, that he was allowing the forces of corruption to dictate the treatment of just men. Valerius knew that his time had run out and he must trust to those who remained, to see Rome restored to those values that had made her great.

In the time he had left he enjoyed their peace and serenity, re-read a couple of well-loved scrolls and had his cook prepare his favourite meals. He'd like to have been able to send a message to Poppaea to reassure her that he'd had no part in naming her, but decided that if he did, he might only make her situation worse.

Valerius' last few days passed very quickly.

In the middle of a glorious day, in his favourite place in the garden, he slit his wrists and died. As expected, when the guards arrived, they found him slumped on the ground in a pool of blood. He loved Rome to the end and had no regrets about his time in her service. His last prayer to the gods was to protect the city from the venom of Messalina.

5

POMPEII

Whispers. Whispers. Whispers.

Poppaea was worried. She'd known for many years that the Empress, Messalina, was jealous of her beauty. Friends had warned her to be careful. Nonetheless, she hadn't expected the evil of which Messalina was now proving herself capable.

Word had reached Poppaea that she'd become the subject of scandalous gossip and insinuations in Rome. It spread like wildfire throughout the bathhouses, bars and public spaces where people stopped on street corners to gossip as the rumours gathered momentum. Some added additional made-up details of their own.

The death of Asiaticus caused a major ripple of excitement but also surprise as he was generally respected by the people. He was known as a pleasant and generous man who had been known to help those in need.

Messalina, wife to the Emperor Claudius, had been scheming to gain possession of former consul Asiaticus' famed pleasure gardens. Poppaea was suspected, so the gossip went, of being an accomplice with Asiaticus in planning a coup, and also having committed adultery with him.

Poppaea knew that all of this was untrue – but proving it would be another matter. In fact, how could she ever really prove it? She sat alone in the garden desperately trying to find a way around the problem. Unless she could stop the scandal that was fast erupting around her, her daughter's reputation would be tainted with her mother's supposed guilt.

There had to be a solution. Tears rolled down her cheeks. She rose and as she walked through to her bedroom, she heard the rain begin to fall. She looked into her daughter's former room as she walked by and knew that whatever the price, she must protect her.

Poppaea was caught in a trap that was not of her own making. It was a tangled web of lies and intrigue caused by the greed of one evil woman. Unfortunately, Poppaea was not in a position to untangle it. Having dressed as simply as possible she sent for her carriage.

'Domina, where do you wish to go?' her driver asked.

'To the evil cesspit that is Rome,' she replied, 'and may I find the strength to do what I must.'

A couple of days later having returned from her journey to visit the poisoner, Locusta, Poppaea bathed and dressed in her best clothes. She attended to her face and her hair, and then sat down to write messages for Poppy and Farzana. She left Farzana's beside her on the bed and that for her daughter in her old bedroom. Carefully picking up the pretty blue vial of liquid that she'd been given, she removed the stopper. Then, she sat on the bed and before she could change her mind drank every drop from the vial. She lay down and waited.

Mercifully, the end was quick and painless.

Poppaea Sabina was dead.

My dear friend, Farzana

Perhaps the rumours may have already reached you about my alleged adultery with Asiaticus. I give you my word that it is not true and that I have committed no act of treason.

You have been a wonderful friend to me.

I ask that you continue your relationship with Poppy. It may be that she will be in need of your friendship more than ever in the days to come.

Farewell, Farzana. You are loyal, loving and compassionate. I thank you from my heart.

Poppaea

My darling daughter,

By the time you read this you will know of the terrible rumours circulating about me. I give you my pledge as your mother that they are not true. I would do anything to be able to make this right, but I cannot fight those with far greater power than myself. I've taken the only way out that I can think of to protect your reputation.

Lorraine Blundell

You are more precious to me than you can ever know.

Surely, one day, the gods will re-unite us. Until then, stay true to the values I have given you. Turn to Farzana who will be a caring friend to you.

Your loving mother,

Poppaea

'Good morning, Poppaea!' Farzana called out cheerfully as she entered the villa only to find a scene of unexpected chaos and mourning. 'What's happened?' she asked Amira who stood before her, tears streaming down her cheeks, her clothing and hair in a state of complete disarray.

'My mistress is dead.'

'But how? Surely no one would have had a reason to kill her,' Farzana gasped.

Amira broke into a renewed bout of crying. 'She took poison, but how can that be?'

Farzana sat down on the nearest couch and tried to think. She'd heard the rumours about Poppaea which had circulated even in Pompeii. There was no other possible answer. Tears filled her eyes. This lovely woman with such a kind heart had been innocent, Farzana was sure of it. Then, her thoughts went to Poppy and she knew that her friend would be inconsolable. She returned home after asking Amira to send a message to her immediately Poppy returned to Pompeii, as Farzana knew she would.

It seemed wrong to Poppy that the day of the funeral was so bright and sunny. She felt sick at heart and her face when she turned to speak to Farzana was gaunt.

'I can't cope with this,' she whispered.

'You will, Poppy. I'll help you. You have the future in front of you and your mother would have wanted you to live it as well as you deserve.'

They walked behind the musicians hired to lead the procession. Poppy had chosen to have lyre and flute players. She felt obliged to also have professional mourners, but felt that a few was enough. Together with friends and neighbours they made their way slowly towards the Street of Tombs outside the Herculaneum Gate. The street was lined with graves and mausoleums.

Poppaea's body had been prepared for burial at the villa immediately before the start of the nine days of mourning. She'd been washed and covered with costly ointments and perfumes and the smell of incense filled the air. Sadly, Poppy entered the family mausoleum with its towering marble columns and nearby bench for the comfort of mourners, then the funeral attendants laid Poppaea to her final rest.

'Please, leave me alone for a few moments.' She nodded to Farzana that she should also go.

Poppy struggled to accept the reality that her mother was dead. Tenderly she caressed her cold cheek and kissed her softly. They had been so close, now she'd lost not only her mother but also her best friend. She couldn't bear to think of her lying here in this silent tomb.

'If it takes me a lifetime they'll pay for this,' she whispered as tears of grief ran down her face. Hatred burned white hot inside her. Her heart hardened and she vowed that she would have revenge on Messalina and take from her and the royal court what was owed to her for her loss.

It was on this day that Poppy changed forever.

A representative had arrived earlier from the Emperor bearing a message of condolence and regret for the death of Poppaea. He was suitably sombre and respectful but Poppy received him with little courtesy, standing coldly silent as he recited Claudius' meaningless, shallow words.

Poppy also had a secret, one that she'd told no one, not even Farzana. She was sure that she was carrying a child.

Her future would consist of a passionate struggle for all of the power and wealth that she could gain for herself and her child, by whatever means necessary.

Fate, however, had a surprise left for her.

One year later, the gods and Asiaticus as well as Poppaea had their revenge. Messalina was executed in the gardens of Lucullus, charged with attempting to organise an uprising and also of adultery while Claudius was away in Ostia. He'd no longer been able to ignore her political interference and blatant promiscuity.

As Messalina was in the middle of writing a petition to Claudius with the assistance of her mother, she was decapitated by a member of the Guard after not taking the option she'd been given to kill herself.

'I don't have the courage to do it!' she'd cried out as the praetorian approached her.

The woman who'd sent so many others to their deaths did not have the inner strength to die with dignity herself.

Poppy's burning hatred for Messalina would never die, but at least she'd had her vengeance on her even if it had been by someone else's hand. But that wasn't enough. It was barely the beginning.

6

ROME

'How *could* you?' Poppy screamed at Rufrius as he entered the house. Her face was contorted with grief and her eyes puffy. Tears streamed down her cheeks. She'd returned to Rome and waited for her husband. 'You could have done something to save her!' She flew at Rufrius, pummelling him with her fists. 'You're commander of the Guard. You didn't even try! I'll never forgive you!' He attempted to hold her but she pulled away from him.

'Poppy, I didn't order the arrest of Asiaticus, I simply carried out my duty. If it wasn't me, it would have been done by someone else. I'm so sorry for your mother's death. I got the message you left for me that you'd gone to Pompeii and I understand your grief. But I didn't start the treason rumours. It was unfortunate that this was my last task before the end

Lorraine Blundell

of my time with the Guard. You do realise, don't you, that I'm required to resign due to our marriage?'

Poppy glared at him. 'I hope you'll be happy with your one and a half million sestercii financial reward and your new role as a senator,' she snapped at him spitefully, 'but it won't bring my mother back!' With that, she strode past him and entered the litter waiting for her in the street. 'You may be interested to know that I'm carrying your child,' she flung at him. 'Also, I intend to divorce you. I'll need the use of this house to live in until I've had the child and I'm ready to leave.'

Rufrius watched in a state of utter shock as the litter pulled away and his heart ached for his loss. He regretted that he hadn't had the power to prevent this whole, sorry situation, but he'd simply done his duty. Perhaps Poppy would see reason after she'd recovered from the severity of her grief, but he doubted it.

Poppy couldn't escape the convention of wearing mourning clothes for the next six months, and out of respect for her mother, she didn't wish to. As it was, her dark clothing was also a constant reminder to whoever saw her of the injustice she'd suffered.

She had a plan but it would take time to set in motion. First, she hired a litter and visited the luxury shops in the basilica near the pantheon. She would need the most expensive stolas, tunics and footwear as well as jewellery that they stocked. She also had kept the few items that remained of her mother's jewellery.

Where she intended to present herself in the future only the best of everything would do. After a couple of hours of intense buying, she billed the lot to an account in Rufrius' name and returned to the house.

Next, she sent for Farzana, promising in her message to reimburse the family for her lost wages, if they would allow her to come to stay with Poppy for an extended period of time. In reality, from this day onwards, she paid Aulus and Marcellus double what Farzana could have earned in Pompeii's forum.

Finally, she began making herself available for invitations to any social gatherings or contacts she could make, especially for after the birth of her child. She found that the general interest and curiosity of most Roman patrician ladies, overcame their natural fear of any repercussions that might follow friendship with the daughter of someone suspected of treason. In fact, she was approached by those who'd been friends of her mother and were now eager to help her.

Then, she settled into the house with Farzana and waited. It was a quiet time that gave them space just for themselves. Rufrius gained permission to return to the Castra Praetoria for accommodation with the Praetorian Guard. His whole life had been turned upside down by the events that had occurred.

At the end of her pregnancy Poppy's son was born and as an appeasement to Rufrius she agreed to name their son after him. He was a happy child and a delight to Farzana who cared for him as Poppy recovered and began to enter social life at the royal court.

Although Poppy tried to persuade Farzana to mix with the city's somewhat less high-class circles so she'd have a place in society where she felt she belonged, the only couple of times she ventured out, she found herself out of her depth and left standing largely unobserved in the shadows.

'I was never meant to be more than what I am,' she told Poppy, who was worried that she wasn't enjoying herself. 'Really, I'm happy. I'll never be one of them. It's enough for me that I enjoy looking after your precious little boy!'

Poppy hugged Farzana and kissed her cheek. 'What would I ever do without you,' she said softly. 'You are the only one who truly knows me.'

Rufrius breathed a sigh of relief as the Castra Praetoria's forbidding grey walls loomed up in front of him. It had been built as a praetorian barracks some way outside the centre of the city, adjacent to the city walls. He'd received both plaudits and scorn since the death of Asiaticus, but mostly he was seen as simply having carried out his orders. Rufrius was pleased to have somewhere to escape to, away from all of the chatter and particularly from his wife. Their marriage was ruined beyond repair.

'So, how long will you be back with us?' his friend, Polio, asked, as Rufrius dumped his bag of possessions on the next bed.

'I wish I knew myself. The truth is I'm at a bit of a loss to know until my divorce and entry to the senate is final. After that, I plan to buy myself a small place in the city.'

'Don't forget who your friends are when you start trotting around showing off that white toga with the purple stripe, will you!' Polio grinned.

'You can be sure of that. Now let me sleep!' Rufrius groaned as he fell onto the bed and a few minutes later lay dreaming of wealth and comfort in his new life to come.

7

The Royal Palace
The Palatine Hill

As the golden light from a rising sun on a new day transformed the greenery outside her window, Acte sat gazing at the tablet in her hand that proclaimed her to be a Roman citizen. The Emperor, Claudius, had called her to see him and wished her well as he changed her life. She would forever be free from the slavery that had entrapped her.

Claudius adopted her and since then, she'd been known as Claudia Acte. She knew that she was fortunate to have caught the eye of the old man from the time she'd arrived at the palace from the slave ship and she was grateful. Acte had been given a small apartment in the palace with the garden outside her window and a roof over her head, as well as food at the palace, for as long as the Emperor lived.

But how long would that be?

Acte's mind was sharp and she'd been alert to palace politics from the time of her arrival. Her benefactor was barely able to function, so she supposed that it wouldn't be long before he fell victim to the power hunger of those around him.

Acte was slight in build with short, brown hair and brown eyes. Her face could be said to be pleasant rather than pretty, but it was the calm, self-assurance of her graceful manner that set her apart. Scooped up in Rome's conquering net in Gaul, she found herself on the slave platform at the major trading centre, Ephesus, where she was purchased by a slaver and sold into service in Rome's royal palace.

It was then that she felt real fear.

She was led with the other slaves down Curetes Street and Marble Road then, finally, the long road to the harbour until tired and hungry, she'd been pushed on board the slave ship at the beginning of a long journey to Rome.

On arrival at the palace she'd been bathed and dressed and given the duties of a serving girl. She was told that she was never to speak unless requested to do so. She'd reflected that life could have been worse, but she'd lost her freedom.

Claudius noticed her one day. He'd called her to him and spoken to her for some time. Now she was free.

It was fortunate that no one paid her much attention. She'd been given no duties, and she could wander almost anywhere in the palace without being noticed. Placing the citizenship tablet on her bed under the pillow, she took the opportunity to wander in the garden, enjoying the early morning sunshine.

Acte found palace life fascinating. She decided to walk quietly through the hallways and see what was happening this morning. One person she didn't want to see, though, was Agrippina. She was the mother of a young man in the court introduced to her as Nero. Acte was immediately attracted to him, but his mother was always around, her voice raised and threatening.

She shuddered. Still, it wouldn't stop her from exploring. After all, the woman barely noticed her, if at all. The business of the royal court was just beginning for the day as Acte found herself in a large room adjacent to one of the reception rooms.

The doors had not yet been shut and she could see visitors as well as Claudius and his niece, Agrippina, settling themselves comfortably. Slowly, Acte tip-toed quietly up to the double doors, where she stood hidden at the side of the opening by the column beside her, next to the wall. She took a peek inside and her glance was drawn to Nero, reclining in comfort just in front of the royal couple.

She'd taken off her sandals and held them in her hand. The marble floor felt refreshingly cool under her feet. For several minutes she stood watching and listening, then a slight sound caused her to turn and look behind her.

Acte jumped as she saw one of the praetorians standing silently watching her. How long he'd been there she had no idea.

He took her by the arm and marched her towards the back of the room. Then, he glared at her.

'My name is Gaius. You're fortunate that I think I know who you are. But just to be sure, what is your name?'

'Claudia Acte.'

'Well, Claudia Acte, what were you doing just now?'

'I was listening. I'm interested in what happens at court,' Acte replied.

'Do you have any idea how much danger you placed yourself in?'

'But I wasn't doing any harm.'

'The people inside that room don't know that. You could have been arrested on any number of charges. Your curiosity will land you in trouble if you keep doing that sort of thing.'

'I'm sorry,' she whispered.

'That's fine. Please leave and don't let me catch you again unless you're authorised to be here.' Gaius watched as she entered the garden and took the path back to her apartment.

His eyes followed Acte until she was out of sight. He smiled slightly, she was young and full of life and she was very graceful. But his warning had not been totally irrelevant. The royal palace could be dangerous for outsiders and even those who were well known. If Agrippina ever caught Acte – he didn't like to think about the probable outcome.

Acte didn't know it then, but Nero had already noticed her.

The royal coach stopped in front of the palace and Agrippina stepped out followed by Nero. His tutor, Seneca, a distinguished senator, was standing not far away, but he was not noticed, so he stood and watched as they walked up the steps and disappeared inside.

Seneca had seen something he didn't like, and it was dangerous. What had happened in that carriage? By the look of Agrippina's clothing, far more than should have. He ran up the steps and headed for Nero's apartment, hoping fervently that he wouldn't find his mother with him.

Seneca's worst fears were realised. He entered to find Agrippina partially undressed. 'May I have a few words,' he asked, his voice low.

Agrippina glared at him.

'It's urgent business of the Empire,' Seneca told her. 'It would be best if we went to your apartment, don't you think?'

Seneca was probably alone in having no fear whatsoever of Agrippina. His reputation amongst the senate and the people would almost certainly protect him, but he was also a man of principle.

Agrippina slammed the doors shut.

'What do you want?' she hissed.

'You know, Agrippina, don't you, that I am fully aware of what you're trying to do with your son.'

'That's none of your business.'

'I'm making it my business. I'm supposed to be caring for the development of my pupil to take the throne of Rome, should that time come, and I have a responsibility to see to his welfare,' Seneca said evenly. 'Do you have any idea what would happen if the people and the senate knew you'd committed incest with your son?'

'I can control them,' Agrippina replied arrogantly. 'I can play them all on a string,' she laughed, 'and I can certainly control Nero.'

'Perhaps, but can you control the praetorians?' Seneca saw by the change in her expression that his words had found their mark. 'If they thought that the crime of incest had been committed you wouldn't survive another day. That would not be tolerated. I'm warning you, Agrippina, do not force my hand!'

'My son must have an outlet for his needs,' she simpered as she answered in a sulky tone.

'Then, we'll find one. I've noticed him glancing at that freed slave serving girl when he thinks that no one is watching,' Seneca continued. 'Perhaps, it should be made easy for them to be together. If she becomes his mistress, then our problem will disappear, I believe.'

Consequently, the two were purposely left alone together several times and Seneca was relieved when they became obvious lovers. Acte would fit the part very well, he congratulated himself.

Acte found herself alone one day with only Nero remaining in the reception room. He looked up and smiled at her. 'I've seen you here recently, have you just arrived?' he asked her.

'Yes.' Acte looked down at her feet.

'Come over here and talk to me,' Nero ordered. 'There's no one I really like to talk to around here.'

Acte approached and he gestured that she should sit on one of the cushions on the floor beside him. She blushed as she looked up at him, which made her look quite pretty.

Their discussion lasted for some time much to the relief of Seneca, who often heard laughter coming from the room when they were together. He took good note of the hours the two of them spent in one another's company and made sure that eventually, they found the opportunity to spend the night in Nero's apartment.

The problem had been solved.

8

Agrippina held the Empire in her hands or so close to it, that it almost made her fingers itch. At least, that's the way she liked to think of it. Nero was still really a boy and easy to manage. Soon, he'd be the Emperor and then Agrippina would bend him to her wishes. She quite enjoyed the thought of wielding the ultimate power in Rome, and that was what was going to happen. Actually, Nero would be Emperor long before he expected. Little did he realise it would be in name only. As to the timing, sometimes a little helping hand in these matters could prove very beneficial.

It was almost time for another visit to Locusta.

Seneca would bear watching, though. This last incident wasn't the first time he'd overstepped the boundaries of his role as tutor to Nero. But for the moment, it was worthwhile to keep him where he was. He had a distinguished reputation and was well respected. The day would come, however, when he'd pay for all of his meddling along the way. It might not be soon, but she'd make sure he eventually did.

Agrippina shuddered with distaste as Claudius slobbered and stuttered his way through each day. Let him enjoy the few days he had left. It was just a matter of time.

If she controlled the Emperor she'd change a few things, Agrippina thought to herself, and there'd be some worried people who'd be sorry they'd been less than pleasant to her. As far as Acte was concerned, she wasn't any threat. Young and inexperienced, she'd have a great deal of growing up to do before she could ever even hope to match Agrippina.

So far, Nero was so pliable it was almost too easy. He adored his mother and even mentioned, quietly of course, that when he became Emperor he'd have coins made with both of their likenesses on them.

How very sweet!

As for his wife, Octavia, she was weak and easy to keep in her place. Agrippina supported her because she could control her. She was too "nice" for her own good. She could very easily be considered boring. Nero came close to totally ignoring her. She obviously annoyed him for whatever reason he never stated. Octavia was very conservative and the perfect Roman matron. Perhaps, that was the root of the problem.

Everything would sort itself out with just a little help. Agrippina had already begun to pull the strings of the major players behind the scenes. She considered the whole thing to be not much different from a puppet theatre.

'What was the main battle strategy used by Julius Caesar at Alesia?' Seneca sat watching Nero as he slouched on a couch fiddling with a lyre. Nero wriggled and a look of annoyance passed over his face.

Silence. Seneca sat and waited him out, as he always did, and the result was always the same. Nero turned to him and blurted out, 'I don't know.'

'But you were supposedly going to study the battle and be ready to answer questions this morning,' Seneca reminded him, his voice a little sharp.

'It's boring. I can't see the point, and I'm not interested in battles,' Nero retorted. 'I've told you, I like poetry, music and the theatre.'

'We've been through this before,' Seneca continued. 'Eventually, you'll be Emperor and you'll be expected to know all of this. You won't be able to converse with the ambassadors from other countries about music!'

'Maybe I will,' he retorted insolently. 'If I'm Emperor then surely I'll decide what I do or don't need to know and what I talk about.' There was a nasty edge to his voice.

Seneca's patience had just about run out.

'Always remember that you can't control what others really think of you, though,' he advised. 'It's dangerous for an emperor to be thought stupid.'

'Don't ever call me stupid!' A flash of anger crossed Nero's face then was quickly veiled. Getting up, he flounced towards the door. 'I'm tired, I'm not doing any more of this today.' He disappeared out of the room without a backward glance.

Seneca rose and headed for his own apartment. Once there he walked out into the gardens and sat alone, thinking. He'd been with Nero for quite a long time, since he'd been only twelve or thirteen years old. Perhaps, he should retire from tutoring him and enjoy time to himself to do more writing and reading.

He'd seriously think about that. It might even be safer for him to reside somewhere else. Capri was nice.

Seneca's mind was suddenly illuminated and his stomach knotted. For a supposedly intelligent man he realised he'd been incredibly stupid. Why hadn't he seen the danger before? He'd been so proud of his prestigious position, not to mention the money that went with it, as well as the fawning of some of his peers, that he'd let his guard down and that was inexcusable!

He wasn't going anywhere.

He knew too much.

Remembering Nero's flashes of sudden anger and Agrippina's downright aggression, he suddenly appreciated the danger he was in. He'd need to work out a strategy or he wouldn't survive. He'd just simply quietly disappear one night never to be seen or heard from again.

The first thing he needed to do was to calm down.

Seneca took a litter from the palace to the Forum. There he found his friend, Petronius, who was just coming out of the Curia. He took one look at Seneca, and guessing correctly that something was seriously wrong, he took his arm and guided him to the banks of the Tiber. There, unheard by anyone, they were able to walk and talk in complete privacy.

'Now, tell me. What's happened?' Petronius asked. 'Obviously, something's really upset you.'

'I believe I may be in serious trouble, if not today, then very soon. I think that my life may even be in danger.'

Petronius frowned. This was more serious than he'd realised. 'Sit with me and explain yourself.'

As Seneca described the revelation of that morning, Petronius became very still and listened closely. By the time his friend had finished, he'd made the decision to give him information that he wouldn't normally have chosen to tell him this early.

'You do realise, don't you that you're not the only one in danger?' Petronius' voice was low and urgent.

Seneca looked puzzled.

'Obviously not,' Petronius added. 'I'm unable to tell you much yet. There are others involved whose anonymity I must protect at all costs.'

Daughter of Pompeii

Seneca's surprise was evident.

By the time the two men had finished speaking, he'd found out that there were other senators becoming more and more hostile to those in the royal palace as time went by. They considered that the power of the senate was being seriously eroded. It wasn't serious yet, but if it became so, they would act to overthrow the Emperor and perhaps, return to a Republic. Claudius was ineffective and not too much of a problem. They didn't think he'd be around much longer anyway.

They hoped that Nero would be a good replacement. But if he wasn't......

'Be more careful at the palace, Seneca, don't upset anyone too much. Be patient and understand that you won't be left alone.' Petronius gave him a reassuring smile.

The two men walked back towards the Forum with Seneca feeling far less isolated and threatened. He shook his head. Obviously, something important and deadly serious had been going on right under his nose and he hadn't even noticed. Either these men were very, very committed or he was losing his grip.

9

Rome revelled in its glory! During this time the Empire approached the height of its growth and wealth, enjoying the transport into the city of luxury goods from every corner of the realm. The smell of power was in the air.

And an old man, unable to command respect sat on the throne of the largest, most prosperous city in the Empire.

Opulence and extravagance defined the city and determined the expectations of royalty and the wealthy while the poor watched in awe. At night, the Emperor's palace sat jewel-like at the very heart of the city's social life. There, it entranced and beguiled in a world of gaiety and over-indulgence.

Invitations had been sent out to those who were considered by the royal court to be deserving. A celebration dinner was to be held at which the Emperor would make an important announcement.

Daughter of Pompeii

When the night of the dinner arrived, a sky sparkling with stars provided a welcoming canopy above the guests, as they looked up to a gentle moon smiling down serenely upon them.

Or so it seemed.

There was a sense of festivity in the air as many of them glimpsed for the first time, ornate fountains gushing pure water and gardens with an abundance of flowers that fragranced the very air they breathed.

Poppy was wearing an expensive gold robe that hinted at her voluptuous figure. Around her neck she wore a necklace of rich green emeralds. As she stepped from her litter she heard the tinkle of laughter. Julia, one of her mother's friends saw her and came over to speak to her.

'You look absolutely incredible.'

'You're kind, Julia,' Poppy murmured. 'Thank you.'

Her friend, an older woman, stared at her, taking in her beauty from her lovely face to the tips of her sandals. Later that evening she remarked to her husband, a senator, that she'd never seen a more stunning-looking woman.

They reclined and dinner was served. Starlings in honey, fried dormice, nightingales' tongues and vegetables including leeks, beans and artichokes appeared on the tables. Fish and other delicacies served with the best quality garum sauce from Pompeii were also offered, to the delight of guests.

Brilliantly coloured peacocks' feathers adorned the main courses. Platters of fresh fruit and figs as well as flavoured milk puddings completed the meal.

Falernian wine flowed freely served in intricately decorated silver cups. More than one guest drank more of it than was wise.

Poppy watched everything happening around her with great interest. She'd never been so close to Claudius before. He appeared anything but royal. Actually, she thought that he looked quite disgusting, especially for an emperor. He was constantly handed a cloth by one of the courtiers with which to wipe away the drool that gathered at the sides of his mouth. Nonetheless, he seemed oblivious to the appearance he projected as a frail, unattractive, bumbling and weak ruler, intent on simply enjoying himself.

Agrippina, his niece, reclined on the lounge beside him almost smothering him with cloying attention. She stayed at his side the whole evening.

This was one of the largest royal dinners Claudius had held. Rumours had been circulating for some time that following the death of Messalina, the Emperor was ready to announce his forthcoming wedding to a third wife, Agrippina, mother of Nero.

As Poppy looked on, she saw Nero and a young man she didn't know approaching Claudius. He seemed on very good terms with both Nero and the Emperor.

'Yes, that's Salvius Otho. I believe he's new to the court. They're close friends,' one woman told her.

There was a short conversation between the three after which the Emperor attempted to stand. His shaky legs could barely support him and he was assisted by the two men at his side. He spoke to those attending in a weak and faltering voice:

> 'I w-w-welcome you all to dine with me and trust that you'll enjoy yourselves. The Empire c-c-continues to grow and bring us great wealth. But I'm sure you'll agree with me that it needs the gentle, guiding hand of an empress. Therefore, I announce tonight that I will w-w-wed this lovely lady, Agrippina, whose ancestry is known to you all.'

Claudius attempted to stretch out his arm as a gesture of welcome to Agrippina, but in doing so lost his balance and nearly fell. There was an audible intake of breath from those watching before Claudius was helped back to his seat and the dinner resumed. Below the level of the good - natured laughter and banter, carefully whispered comments went unheard, except into the ears of those for whom the comments were intended, but also others who were secretly listening:

> *Agrippina will be giving the commands before long.*
> *Maybe Claudius will have a little accident soon.*
> *The gods help us if ever she gains complete power.*

The guests watched the Emperor and each other, not realising that they in turn, were being watched themselves. Praetorian commander, Afranius Burrus, who'd replaced Rufrius, looked on unseen, as did members of the Guard who wore the plain tunics of servants. They all carried concealed weapons. After all, one never knew when they'd be needed.

The Guard were also there to listen for any treasonous comments they could overhear. They were seemingly innocuous 'slaves' who were, as was the case with all slaves, invisible in the eyes of those around them.

10

The Palatine Hill
Three years later

Finally, the time had come! Locusta squatted down on the dirt floor of the hut and rocked backwards and forwards in delight. She would now have all of the gold she needed to buy herself a house – and not just any house! Her eyes misted over as she saw in her imagination a charming home on the Aventine. A messenger had just left after giving her an order from the Empress, Agrippina, as well as the promise of a large number of gold coins.

She'd taken long enough to act, in the poisoner's opinion. Locusta had plenty of work to do, there was always someone who needed to be poisoned, but this job would pay much more than any other.

She would need to be smart. There was very real risk this time should she not succeed.

For some reason, images of Poppaea flittered back inside her head. It was a pity about that one, Locusta frowned, she was a very beautiful woman, but she'd been in deep despair.

It was time to get to work.

But, what poison to use and how to carry out the act successfully?

The food tasters were the problem with royalty and patricians. She couldn't think why they would place themselves in danger by doing such a task. It made no sense. Then, it occurred to her that perhaps they had no choice.

It was common knowledge that there was one delectable treat that the Emperor couldn't ever resist - mushrooms. Would he wait long enough for the food taster to do his work and fall down dead? Or would his greed get the better of him?

One never really knew.

Several days later, after many gold coins brought by a trusted messenger had clinked into her grimy hand, Locusta provided a bag containing the poison. Inside was an unsigned note which read:

> **Soak the potion into the mushrooms before they are offered to be eaten. If death does not happen immediately, a feather covered with the poison should be used to tickle the throat of the victim as he struggles to breathe. This will result in certain death without suspicion.**

'You understand that this is to be given by hand to the Empress and no one else, don't you!' Locusta emphasised to the messenger. She had no intention of being executed because of someone else's mistake.

'That is my understanding. I'm her personal messenger,' he replied firmly.

'Salve,' Locusta whispered to him as he left the hovel. 'May you travel safely.'

Dinner was a small affair with only Claudius, Agrippina and a few others present. So far, the evening had been pleasant with everyone relaxed and friendly.

Claudius' eyes lit up when he saw a platter of his favourite mushrooms being placed on the table. As the food taster, Halotus, reached out his hand to take a sample, Claudius waved him away.

'These look good enough to eat!' he joked and everyone laughed obligingly.

Claudius scooped up a large spoonful from the platter and ate them greedily. Moments later, he collapsed and fell to the floor but was still alive. Agrippina played her part like the murderer she was.

'Quickly, get me a feather!' she yelled as if in a panic.

By pre-arrangement, Locusta, hidden in the next room, handed a feather dipped in poison to a bribed courtier who hurried to the table.

'Hold his mouth open!' Agrippina ordered. Clutching the feather, she pushed it into Claudius' mouth and down his throat as far as it would go. He shook and foamed at the mouth as chaos broke out around him.

Within minutes he was dead. Nero would be Emperor.

The Tullianum Prison

The sinister prison adjacent to the senate house in the Forum, was not a place where people tended to loiter. Most passed quickly by it or avoided it altogether, glad that they were outside its walls. It was usually a place of temporary confinement prior to execution.

The prison was so ancient most citizens couldn't ever remember not seeing it there. After the Triumphs held in the city to celebrate the deeds of Rome's victorious generals, it was usual procedure for rulers of conquered states to be executed in the prison when the procession had reached its end.

This was where Locusta found herself. She'd been implicated in the murder of Claudius.

I knew this would happen, but it's worth it. The next emperor or someone close to me will need my skills before long, and they'll remember me. All I have to do is keep my mouth shut, say nothing and wait.

Locusta grunted.

Inside the prison was dim with filthy walls that were damp in winter. Down a narrow, twisting flight of steps was the execution chamber. It was even smaller and darker than the area above, and the sound from water flowing through the underground sewer was ever present.

Locusta crouched on the floor of the prison where she'd been confined, charged with providing poison to kill Claudius. No one could deny she was skilled in the use of poisons. In some ways, such as now, though, her brilliant reputation was not an asset.

She supposed that every type of work had its drawbacks.

Locusta wondered what the law court would say, if it knew that she'd also lately committed another murder of an unusually important nature. It was probably best that they didn't know, she concluded.

Nero had a brother, Britannicus.

He no longer had a brother now.

No one knew that he'd been poisoned, convinced that he'd had a fit of some kind. After all, he hadn't even eaten any food before he collapsed.

A look of pride crossed the poisoner's face.

Challenged by the knowledge that her own fate would be sealed if she'd failed to kill him, Locusta tried something a little different from the usual poisoning.

During dinner the fatal potion had been added to the water instead of the food. Britannicus drank when he was offered water from the amphora, because what was already in his cup was far too hot. That was his fatal mistake.

Locusta hoped that somehow, she'd soon be released. What most people didn't know, was that she was undeniably tough and also very patient. Her prophesy proved correct. It was only a couple of weeks later, that she was granted her freedom again.

As long as Nero was in power, she knew she was relatively safe. She also knew that she'd always have work. Beyond that was too far in the future to worry about.

11

BAIAE

South of Rome
Villa of Lucius Calpurnius Piso

Poppy breathed deeply, appreciating the freshness of the salty sea air. Her gaze swept the sea in front of her, lingering on the slaves working on the oyster lines further along the coastline. Baiae was the ultimate luxury playground of royalty and the social elite. She'd heard about it but the poor and people of minor status such as herself never caught so much as a glimpse. Now she knew why.

This was very much a closed social setting.

'It's absolutely magnificent,' she murmured.

Linked to Rome by the deep harbour of Puteoli nearby, a good road, the Via Herculania, also joined the two places for the supply of goods, but Baiae was short of much needed fresh water. This was available, however, thanks to the Aqua Augusta coming from Rome.

'Brilliant, isn't it!' Poppy turned at the sound of Salvius Otho's voice. 'We're fortunate to be staying by invitation, at Calpurnius Piso's waterfront villa. It's the most luxurious here. Even the Emperor's next door can't match it.'

Poppy smiled up at him. 'This is so exciting. Will I meet the Emperor while I'm here?'

'I was going to keep it a secret, but now that you mention it, we are. We're invited to dinner with Nero tomorrow night.'

Poppy's eyes sparkled with happiness. Now she was really on her way to where she wanted to be. A 'chance' meeting recently with Salvius had led to a relationship with him and she'd found it easy to lead him wherever she wanted to.

'Would you like to see the rest of the villa?' Salvius asked, pleased that Poppy seemed so impressed.

'I certainly would!' she laughed and linked her arm with his. He looked decidedly happy.

She was stunned as they walked from room to room as she mentally calculated the huge amount of wealth that had been spent here by Piso. Wonderful wall frescoes using many colours, including expensive blues and greens, caught her attention as well as dancing golden cupids. Lamp stands gave off a luminous light in rooms which were spacious, with most facing the sea.

As dusk fell, they wandered the extensive gardens as the flares were lit, admiring the many statues that decorated them. Their last stop was at the stone theatre built into the cliff behind it. With her back to it facing the sea, as dusk fell, Poppy felt a sense of elation. Never had she been in a place so beautiful.

For once, she was caught by surprise. Salvius knelt on the grass before her and took her hand.

'Will you marry me?' he asked, looking up at her.

'I'd like a little more time,' Poppy hesitated. 'I feel that I need to get to know you better. May I give you my answer before we leave?'

Salvius' expression fell a little, then he forced himself to smile. 'Of course,' he answered, 'I understand that it's an important decision for you.'

'It's very much my honour!' Poppy flattered him as they walked slowly back towards the villa. Her head was in a spin. His offer of marriage had come sooner than expected.

Poppy slept well that night lulled into a sense of relaxation by the sound of the sea and a feeling that her plan was working like a dream. By morning, she'd made up her mind. She would, however, make Salvius wait a day or two before telling him what she'd decided.

The next morning she went alone to the villa baths. The space and luxury astounded her. Slowly, she slipped into the frigidarium pool, gazing at the surroundings. Lining the perimeter were niches in which stood life-size marble statues, and she could hear the hissing of the steam from Baiae's encircling volcanoes that heated the nearby sauna.

Poppy knew that no matter what it took, she must have this lifestyle and she'd pay just about any price to get it.

'No!' Poppy snapped at the slave sent to help her. 'That's not the way I want it!' She flung the hairpin down on the table. Her nerves were on edge tonight, for once, she was nervous. She heartily wished that she'd brought Farzana with her. Then she wouldn't have to explain to some stupid slave how to do her hair. After all, it wasn't that complicated.

Poppy had decided to wear her long, deep blue robe. With it she wore pearl earrings set in gold. Unless the mirror was lying to her, she knew that she looked as lovely as ever.

Her confidence rose even higher when Salvius entered the room. He appeared to be virtually speechless until, finally, he spluttered, 'You look unbelievably beautiful!'

'Thank you,' she smiled. 'It's time, I believe, to join the Emperor for dinner.'

'Before we go, I should tell you that Nero's mistress will be there.'

'Is that the girl they call Acte?' Poppy asked.

'Yes. She arrived here as a slave at the palace and Claudius liked her so much that he adopted her.'

'Really. He adopted her?' Poppy echoed in disbelief.

'I've been told that's what happened.' Salvius shrugged his shoulders. 'I don't really know anything much about her.'

'So, how does Nero's mother feel about it?'

'Agrippina's furious! She's very fond of Nero's wife, Octavia. She's been trying to impress on Nero that the people love her and he's lucky to have her as his empress. So far, it's not working. I think that the situation is going to become very difficult, but we shouldn't let it spoil our evening. Anyway, I'll tell you more about it all later.' He linked his arm with Poppy's and together they made their way to dinner, using the path at the top of the clifftop to Nero's imperial villa next door.

'Come and join us!' Nero invited them with a sweeping motion of his arm. 'I'm told that dinner will be ready shortly.' He gestured towards a couch adjacent to the one on which he reclined. His mistress he'd placed on the other side of him.

Poppy smiled at Nero as she and Salvius reclined as suggested. She risked a quick look at the woman opposite who was reclining looking relaxed. She was young, with a sweet face rather than a pretty one.

'That's Acte. I don't believe you know her,' Nero continued, having seen Poppy's glance. He added no further information as Acte nodded politely to Poppy.

'You may play,' Nero ordered the musicians who were standing silently to the side. 'But keep it soft, I don't want to have to shout at my guests.'

It ran through Poppy's mind, having heard the stories about Nero's love of playing music, that he might play tonight himself. She was slightly disappointed and her curiosity was left unresolved, as he didn't seem inclined to do so at the moment.

'How are you both enjoying the hospitality of Calpurnius' villa?' Nero looked directly at Poppy.

'It's very beautiful, Caesar.'

'I hope that you don't prefer it to what you've seen so far of mine,' he stated, arching an eyebrow.

Before Poppy could reply, Salvius answered quickly, 'that wouldn't be possible, Caesar, as yours definitely has the preferred position on the clifftop.'

Nero beamed at them as the first dishes were brought to the table. 'Do try the oysters, they're the finest in the Empire. Those you see in front of you were taken from the sea only this morning, and did you notice the large fish pond on my estate?'

Dinner progressed in a relaxed manner, the conversation being kept to everyday matters of no real importance. As they rose to leave, Nero turned towards Salvius.

'May I borrow your guest for a couple of minutes?'

'Of course, Caesar,' he replied obligingly.

Nero took Poppy by the hand and led her to the balcony facing the sea. 'There is no more stunning view anywhere in the Empire, don't you agree?'

'It's beyond description. I've never seen a more beautiful place,' Poppy replied honestly, her face close to his.

'I'm so pleased you like it!' Nero squeezed her hand.

They returned to join Salvius and Acte.

'Why don't you both come with us tomorrow to the Temple of Mercury to bathe. It's quite an experience,' Nero suggested.

'It would be our pleasure,' Salvius agreed. As they left the room Poppy felt Nero's eyes on her back until they'd gone. It was then, also, she realised that Acte had not said one word during the whole evening.

The next morning Poppy awoke to brilliant sunshine. She looked out at a sparkling sea and suddenly became aware of the silence. Gone was the cacophony of noise arising each day from the daily living of Rome's people. She resolved to make the most of every minute in Baiae. She hurried to dress so as to be ready in time for the outing to the temple.

'Lady, may I enter with your breakfast?' one of the slaves requested shortly after.

'Enter.'

Poppy took a plate of fruit and ate it as she admired the view from the balcony of her room. She could see the fishing boats out early catching the seafood to be served that night. Soon, she was finished and dressed just as she heard Salvius' voice.

'Poppy, it's time to leave. We mustn't keep the Emperor waiting.'

'Do you know the way?' she asked as they left the villa.

'Yes. I'm afraid it's a climb from here, but it's not too difficult.'

As they walked, Poppy looked around at the wildflowers growing in profusion beside the narrow path as well as the many herbs. The fresh tang of the sea melded with their fragrance in a heady mix. She knew that this truly was paradise on earth.

It wasn't long before they reached the huge half dome squatting on the ground. Known as the Temple of Mercury it was an enclosed bathing pool. As they approached, they were greeted by praetorians guarding the entrance.

'Welcome! The Emperor bids you enter.

Nero and Acte were preparing to enter the pool as Salvius and Poppy reached them. She looked around her at the huge space with an oculus at the top and open windows cut into the sides to allow sunlight to spill inside.

'Salve, Caesar and Acte,' Poppy and Salvius greeted them both and their hosts returned their greeting with a welcome.

Daughter of Pompeii

'Come into the water with us. The temperature is absolutely perfect.'

Their voices echoed throughout the temple as they all began to swim and splash in the natural thermal pool, one of many that occurred due to the twenty-four volcanoes that ringed the town. They laughed and played in the water like children their voices ringing out in a hollow echo, and it seemed as if the outside world no longer existed.

Time ceased to matter and the morning disappeared into what seemed like a whirlpool. Eventually, Nero and Acte left to return to the imperial villa.

'Would you like to go back?' Salvius asked as he and Poppy were dried off by attending slaves.

'Not yet, I don't think,' she replied. 'Why don't we take a walk along the beach and have a look at the oyster farm?'

They walked slowly hand in hand feeling the sand scrunching between their toes and when they reached the men tending the oysters, they were offered a sample each.

The oysters were plump and straight from the sea. There were none better in the Empire.

As they turned to return to their villa, Poppy reached a decision. There was no point in prolonging revealing it, she decided.

'I will marry you,' Poppy told Salvius as they sat alone for a few minutes on the beach watching the huge, red sun sink slowly below the horizon.

'You have given me a prize beyond measure.' He kissed her tenderly. 'We must tell Nero.'

While Nero slept, Acte left the imperial villa and walked to an isolated area of the beach. She sat on the verge of the sand staring at the sea, broken-hearted. She'd seen Nero's intense interest in the woman who'd come to dinner. Acte was still young but she was realistic enough to realise that there was no way she could compete with the beautiful woman who'd accompanied Otho.

She knew that she'd never be more to Nero than a mistress due to her very low social status. It was only because of her adoption by Claudius that this link she had with him was even possible. As an enslaved mime actress from Asia brought to Rome to serve at the royal palace, she'd captured the old emperor's heart.

Tears welled up in her eyes and spilled down onto her cheeks. She'd been with her lover for some years and thought that the worst was over when she'd won against his mother, Agrippina, a monster of a woman who'd tried to seduce her own son, and was stopped only by the determination of the senator, Seneca, to deter her, because of the scandal that would surely follow.

Octavia was still empress. That left only the role of mistress. Acte had noticed that she'd been called to the Emperor's apartment less and less, recently. Time for her was running out and when it did, she'd made up her mind that she'd go quietly.

Nero had been generous.

Acte was a wealthy woman in her own right with estates in Velitrae and Sardinia. If she looked hard enough, it was almost possible from where she sat to see the estate she owned across the water in Puteoli. She'd never asked for anything from him but he'd loaded her with gifts.

She had genuinely loved Nero for years and tried to give him good counsel especially now he was Emperor. Lately, though, it seemed to her that he'd changed. The goodwill that he'd lavished earlier on the senate had become less and less, leading to a growing sense of hostility.

Acte knew deep down that her dream was almost over.

Nero did not send for her again in the weeks that followed and soon after she left the palace. She spent the final morning sitting alone near her favourite statue of Juno in the tiny garden that bordered her small apartment. Even then, she continued to vacillate about her decision but in the end, she accepted that it had to be this way.

Acte lived in her estate at Velitrae after that day, but remained loyal to Nero, closely following all the news from Rome.

Part II

'Living well is the best revenge'

George Herbert

12

ROME

The Royal Palace
The Palatine

Poppy walked swiftly along the darkening colonnade, her sandals slapping hollowly against the hard paving stones as she walked. Her arrival would, unfortunately, be less discrete than she'd hoped. The evening was turning cool and she wished she'd brought her shawl. The gold earrings she wore swung to the rhythm of her walk, echoing her anxiety of mind. Although Nero's summons to attend him at his apartment was far from unexpected, now that the moment had come, she felt surprisingly nervous.

The guards allowed her to continue as she passed them, walking down the long passageways and across marble floors.

In the imminent darkness, she could just make out through the windows the magnificent statues reposing amidst trees and fountains. Flares cast pools of light onto pathways and benches, leaving corners of half hidden mystery.

Eventually, one of the guards stopped her and she was led into an anteroom adjacent to the Emperor's bedroom. The attendant inside left the room and she found herself alone. She didn't have long to wait.

'So, we meet again. Thank you for coming.'

Poppy turned at the sound of his voice to see Nero standing in the doorway to the inner bedroom. She found that her mouth was dry and licked her lips before attempting to answer.

'It is an honour, Caesar,' she managed to say.

'Come here.'

She went to him and they walked further into the bedroom together, his arm around her waist. He turned her to face him so he could look at her.

'I've been thinking of you since Baiae, I believe it's time we became closer.'

Poppy stood rigid under his touch as he began stripping away her clothes. She was to discover that night, that Nero was not a gentle lover.

Over the months that followed she was constantly in his bed. Her new husband, Otho, heard nothing of the affair which was kept tightly secret. Then, without warning, three months later he was called to the palace.

Something didn't seem right, he thought, as he walked the silent passages at the end of an anxious day worrying. He hadn't seen Nero since he'd been with him at Baiae. Certainly, everything had been especially friendly then. Perhaps, Nero had some pleasant surprise for him. Still, anxiety nagged at him as he approached the study to which he'd been directed.

The praetorians guarding the door parted to allow him to enter. He did so, trying to appear confident.

Daughter of Pompeii

'Come, my friend,' Nero greeted him, as the commander of the Guard, Tigellinus, looked on. 'I think you're wasted here in Rome. I need loyal men to govern Rome's provinces so I've decided to send you to Lusitania.'

Otho stood speechless.

'Surely, you're pleased with my faith in you?' Nero smiled upon seeing the complete and utter shock on Otho's face.

'Yes, Caesar, but what about Poppy?'

'You don't need to worry about her,' Nero stated.

'You'll divorce her and she'll stay here where she's safe. You leave in three days. That is all. You may go.'

Otho felt as if his feet were nailed to the floor. Desperately, he tried to mentally frame some defence to Nero's wishes, but in vain.

Tigellinus snapped to attention and walked to stand beside Otho, who found himself being smartly marched from the room and shown the palace door after a firm pat on the back from the praetorian commander.

Poppy moved into the palace. She was given an apartment near that of Nero and she loved it. Frequently, she was by Nero's side rather than Octavia, except where royal protocol demanded the attendance of the Empress for matters of state, such as audiences for visiting ambassadors.

She had never before lived in the luxury that filled her days as the Emperor's favourite. Acte had gone and there was no sign she'd be returning, so Poppy had no fear she'd be replaced. Relaxed and confident, she was outgoing in advising Nero on affairs of state in the hearing of others.

Poppy's apartment opened out to the gardens. It was private and furnished with luxury. She ran her fingers along the edge of a priceless side table purchased from the east of the Empire. At her request, to remind her of Pompeii, she'd had the gardeners plant roses in the garden beds and vases of them were placed in her apartment each morning.

'I think the green one today, Farzana,' she smiled as she prepared to dress. A small apartment next to her own had been given to Farzana for her use. Beautifully furnished with rugs from Asia and silken bed linens, it looked out onto the side of the rose garden.

'And the silver sandals, perhaps today?' Farzana suggested softly.

'That's a good choice.'

Farzana was awed by her apartment and her presence grounded Poppy, calming her and giving her the confidence she needed to live this life she'd chosen.

Poppy sat and glanced across at her friend. 'Have you ever wondered why I've devoted all my energy to reaching where I am today?'

'No.' There was a slight smile on Farzana's lips. 'I've always known. But now you have your revenge, will this be enough for you?'

'You know me too well,' Poppy laughed. 'I intend to enjoy what I've earned for as long as I can. If that leads me to greater power, I won't complain. As for revenge, I don't believe that is quite over yet.'

'I'd like to ask if you'd allow me to visit Pompeii soon?' Farzana suggested.

'I'm sorry, I didn't realise that you were homesick. How selfish of me. You've been by my side for so long.'

'It's not that,' Farzana continued. 'My father's quite old now and I'd never forgive myself if I didn't at least try to see him.'

'Then, of course you must go!' Poppy stood and walking over to Farzana, held her close. 'I can never repay your loyalty to me, and I trust you know how grateful I am. I do hope, though, that you'll come back.'

They walked out together to recline on couches on the portico beside the flowers. Poppy called for drinks for them both, and it wasn't long before she smiled to see that the garden had enticed Farzana into the realm of sleep, hopefully with pleasant dreams. To the watching eyes of a stranger, it would have been obvious that this close relationship would last forever.

The next day Poppy entertained with Nero in one of the large rooms of the palace. A few of the Emperor's friends joined them casually to discuss the affairs of the Empire. Their laughter was easy and unforced and Nero seemed particularly carefree. They were enjoying the platters of food and cups of wine for a light lunch, when without warning, Agrippina swept into the room.

'Octavia has just told me that you cancelled your lunch appointment with her,' she confronted Nero aggressively. Agrippina glared at Poppy. 'I would think you would enjoy her company more than those present!'

'Mother, why can you not attempt to be pleasant when you can see that I have guests?' Nero snapped irritably.

Agrippina ignored his question.

'And I see that you've dismissed Acte in favour of this cheap, ambition-driven woman!' She pointed her finger directly at Poppy who managed to look offended even though she knew Agrippina couldn't really hurt her.

'At least Acte cared for you, she continued. 'She didn't deserve to be pushed aside for this newcomer. If you must have a mistress call Acte back!'

Furious, Nero strode quickly over to her and shook her hard. 'You will apologise. Now!'

'Don't make me laugh! I put you where you are. You'd be nothing but an upstart without me.'

Nero's rage boiled over and he shoved her hard to the floor. Raising herself to her feet Agrippina pulled back her arm and hit him across the face as hard as she could.

'Tigellinus!' Nero roared.

He strode quickly into the room, aware of the argument he'd heard through the door. 'Caesar!'

'My mother is never to be admitted again to the palace or to my presence. Go!'

He walked over to Poppy to comfort her. On his face was a red hand imprint from where his mother had struck him.

Even as she left the room, Agrippina had a smirk on her face. She departed the palace immediately for her country estate in Misenum. From there, she did as much damage as possible to Nero's reputation by spreading untrue rumours to anyone who would listen.

Agrippina still had spies at court who reported back to her in the hope that she would rise again in power and reward them. Her country estate was impressive with a view of the sea. She could afford to wait. This drama was a long way from finished.

13

In her apartment Octavia was attempting to read one of the many petitions sent to her by Rome's citizens. She sighed and placed them on the desk in front of her. She was restless. She hadn't sought to be empress but felt that she'd had no choice when Agrippina insisted that she marry Nero. Octavia wasn't particularly ambitious and would have been just as happy as a Roman matron of comfortable means with a husband and children.

Nero had ignored her from the very beginning and had never slept with her. In vain, she waited night after night for him to visit her apartment. Consequently, they were childless. That was what caused her real sadness. At least, if she'd had a child she'd feel as if she had a purpose in life.

Was she at fault, she wondered, for not being more demanding? But that was not in her nature. The question recurred in her mind, 'how does one force an emperor to treat his wife with respect and to genuinely care about her?'

She'd not yet found the answer to that question.

Today, she would attend another charity event. Her presence at such times was expected as part of her royal duties. This time, it was to raise funds for the rebuilding of the temple of Bona Dea on the Aventine. Those attending, only women, were of high social class. The goddess was revered by the matrons of Rome who held her in great esteem but the temple had begun to show its age and was in need of repairs. They constantly annoyed their husbands with requests for donations until they gave in purely to get some peace. Even so, more money was needed.

'Order my carriage, please,' Octavia requested one of her slaves. 'I will be leaving soon for the Aventine.'

'Yes, Domina.'

Concerns plagued her mind as she travelled in silence to the temple. Once there, she put on her best smile and gave the ladies waiting for her exactly what they expected. Gracious and smiling, Octavia moved amongst them praising them for their efforts for the temple.

Little did she realise how many of Rome's people, rich and poor, had grown to love her for her kindness and gentleness, but she would soon find out.

Pompeii

Farzana was in a fluster preparing for her journey to Pompeii. Poppy laughed as she saw her checking everything at least twice so she wouldn't forget anything.

'You will be all right without me to help you, Poppy, won't you?' Farzana asked again.

'Of course. And I can always use someone from the palace staff if I have to,' Poppy smiled at her indulgently. 'I know it's not the same, but I'm sure I can manage.

Daughter of Pompeii

Farzana, I have a gift here for you to give your father from me and also another for Marcellus. Also, here is a purse of coins. I want you to use them for your expenses.'

Finally, it was time for Farzana to leave. She hugged Poppy and they walked down the corridor to the side door where one of Poppy's carriages waited.

'Goodbye, Farzana, be safe. Don't forget to come back to me!' Poppy stood waving to her friend until the carriage disappeared into the distance.

The journey was long and Farzana was exhausted by the time she reached Napoli. Using some of the coins Poppy had given her she stayed overnight at one of the decent accommodation inns in a narrow, cobbled street. It was noisy but clean and no one bothered her. Her excitement rose at the thought of seeing her father and brother again so she woke early the next morning to make an early start to the final part of her travel. She barely caught more than a glimpse of the city's beautiful bay as she left.

The carriage bumped along until, finally, she entered through the city walls and was surprised to find Pompeii looking so tawdry now that she was back. Then, she realised that it was she who'd changed, not the city. What did surprise her was how strong her emotions were now that she was actually home. She felt as if she'd been away for years, then she laughed as she remembered that she actually had.

'Here we are!' the driver said as he climbed down from his horse to get her belongings for her. 'This is Via Consolare.'

'Thank you. It's good to be back.'

Marcellus and Aulus heard her arrival and came rushing through the door of the house. Farzana fell into their arms laughing and crying at the same time.

'Come in. There's so much to catch up on,' Marcellus urged her as he brought her bags inside.

The little house felt so very small to Farzana.

They were tired by the time all the gossip, news and happenings had been sifted through and discussed. By the time she fell into bed in her old bedroom, Farzana had a calm look on her face and found herself uncertain as to whether she ever wanted to leave again.

After a leisurely breakfast she dressed in comfortable clothes and shoes. Aulus had already opened the shop and was attending to a customer as she was ready to leave.

'I'll be out having a look around,' Farzana told him as she stepped out of the door. There was one private thing that she wanted to do first.

With a wry smile, she bought a bunch of colourful flowers from one of the sellers in the forum, paying more than the price of the flowers, for which she received warm thanks from the girl. Heading through the Herculaneum Gate she entered the street of tombs. It was a sad place but no one could be buried inside the city walls, so there was no other choice but to place the dead together here.

She found Poppaea's mausoleum easily and sat down on the bench beside it to remember the death of Poppy's mother. She'd been a lovely woman and Farzana still missed her.

'May you be at peace,' she whispered as she laid the flowers down. 'I miss you.'

Soon, she turned and wandered back through the city walls. Walking down Via Stabiana through the crowd she could see the brilliantly coloured Basilica, and felt a strange flutter in her heart as she finally reached her destination adjacent to the Via Marina. Farzana had come back today to visit the garden of the Temple of Venus again.

That was always the place she thought of as 'belonging' to herself and Poppy. At the moment, it was deserted.

At first, she simply stood and looked at the temple. Built on a podium surrounded by a portico, its marble gleamed in the sun. She could see the houses of the priests of the goddess further down the slope of the hill.

Making her way into the garden grove, Farzana sat down and reflected on how much her life as well as Poppy's had changed since they'd been here so many years before. The twists and turns of fate would have astounded them had they known what the future held.

Finally, she shook herself free from the past, and realising that she was hungry, went to the nearby thermopolium, where she purchased a bowl of beef stew and a cup of wine. As she walked home, she stopped on Via di Nola to buy bread for their meal that night.

'How long will you be staying in Pompeii?' Aulus asked Farzana the following morning.

'I don't have any set time to return to Rome,' she answered.

'I wish you weren't going back,' he confided in her. 'With all of us together again it's really wonderful.'

Farzana came up behind him and put her arms around his neck. 'I know,' she said softly as she kissed him, 'I missed you, that's why I came back. I'll have to make a decision soon as to whether I'll return to Rome, but it's going to be difficult. Anyway, I'm going out this morning to have a better look around Pompeii. I should be home for a late lunch.'

Taking a couple of the coins from her purse, she left and walked towards the forum. She thought perhaps she might find a small gift to give her father. She didn't like to see him sad. As she arrived at the macellum in the forum she saw that a fight had broken out. Two men were brawling on the ground and soon the violence spread with others joining in.

Two praetorians on horseback from the nearby Nuceria barracks rode over and soon had the fight under control. Farzana had been watching with the rest of the passers-by when she realised that one of the praetorians was studying her closely.

'Lady, stop!' he called out as she started to move away.

Farzana stood absolutely still, petrified with fear, as she wondered what she'd done wrong. The praetorian dismounted and came to face her.

'Salve! My name is Aeneus Capito. I'm a trooper with the tenth praetorian cohort,' he told her. Your face is familiar to me but I can't think why. What's your name?'

'Farzana,' she answered him.

'Now I remember! I met you one day when I accompanied commander Crispinus to where you were staying on the Aventine in Rome. I presume you know that Agrippina had him executed later?'

Farzana's face turned pale.

'No. I didn't know.'

'It was a sad business that happened a few years ago now. He was a great commander. The men liked him, but apparently Agrippina didn't. She got rid of him to put someone of her own choice in that position. Apparently, she thought that Rufrius was too much under the influence of the previous Empress, Messalina.'

'I liked him. I'm sorry,' Farzana said, genuinely shocked.

'Obviously you're now living in Pompeii. Are you no longer in contact with the girl who was commander Crispinus' wife?' Aeneus asked.

Farzana nodded. 'I am, but I was also born here and I've returned to see my family. I still visit her as often as I can, but it's difficult.' She felt eager to change the subject.

'I'd really like to meet you again if you'd agree,' Aeneus suggested, removing his helmet.

'I'd like that too.'

'What about if you give me your address and I'll pick you up. I have close friends in Stabiae. A visit to see them should be entertaining,' he finished, with a grin.

Aeneus replaced his helmet, mounted his horse and rode out of the forum with his companion. Farzana stared after him. He was young with a nice smile and respectful towards her.

Farzana could think of worse ways to spend a day than in his company.

The next day Aeneus turned up at Farzana's house where he met Aulus. Farzana thought how splendid he looked in his praetorian uniform but her father seemed a little awed. Nonetheless, he asked questions about their destination for the day.

'Where are you two going?"

'I have friends who own a villa at Stabiae. It's a spectacular seaside resort. It's not far away at all.'

'I'd like that,' Farzana commented.

'Don't worry, I'll look after her,' Aenus assured Aulus as they left.

'They all say that,' he replied cynically.

'But I'm a praetorian,' Aeneus assured him confidently.

Aulus raised an eyebrow. 'Then, I suppose I'd better take you at your word!'

They spoke about the royal court, Aenus' praetorian duties and the gossip that flooded through it, as the carriage rattled along the short distance on the country road to Stabiae.

Three magnificent villas stood on the headland above a bay. They lay under the very shadow of Vesuvius as they watched the sun come up over a choppy sea.

'It is a stunning place!' Farzana said admiringly.

'And you haven't even seen inside my friend's villa yet,' Aeneus laughed.

'I can't believe it's one of these three!' Farzana exclaimed as the carriage finally managed to reach the top of the headland and pulled up outside one of them.

A tall man with short, dark hair, came to greet them. 'It's wonderful to see you again, Aeneus,' he clapped him on the back, 'It's been too long. And how delightful that you have a guest with you!' He led them inside into the cool villa interior. 'We did get your message so we've been expecting you.'

A pretty, petite woman came forward to meet them. 'I'm Irena, welcome. I suppose my husband forgot to tell you his name,' she said with embarrassment after being introduced to Farzana.

'It's Sextus,' he grinned.

Farzana laughed more that afternoon than she had for a very long time. Their hosts were warm and welcoming with a good sense of humour. As Aeneus glanced at her from time to time, he couldn't help but notice how very pretty Farzana was, especially when she smiled. She wasn't beautiful in the classical way, but she was someone he thought he could become close to.

After lunch, Aeneus and Poppy went for a stroll along the beach. He took her hand and laughed with her as they skipped between the waves.

'I had no idea that Stabiae was so very close to the mountain,' Poppy commented as she looked up at it.

'You're right. The story goes that it blew up a long, long time ago, but I don't think we need to worry,' Aeneus assured her.

Reluctantly, they returned to Pompeii. Aeneus fondly looked into her eyes as they enjoyed a romantic flirtation in the carriage before eventually reaching Farzana's house.

'Did you enjoy yourself?' Aeneus asked hopefully as the carriage arrived at the door.

'I really did and I liked your friends very much,' Farzana answered.

'Well, young man, I'm pleased to see you've kept your word,' Aulus greeted them on their return as Aeneus helped Farzana down and he came to the door.

'Yes, sir. I'd like to take Farzana to the stadium to watch the gladiator games in a couple of days. Would that be acceptable?'

'I've got no objection. But, be sure you look after her well. The games can become a bit rough at times.'

It was, perhaps, a good thing that Aulus couldn't see into the future. What he did know was that Farzana seemed to be glowing.

14

It was a good day for fighting. Warm and sunny but with a cooling breeze, it drew many of the citizens of Pompeii out to watch the gladiator bouts. There was a very long tradition of rivalry between the Pompeii Reds and nearby Nuceria Blues. Crowds streamed in through the city gate, mainly coming from Nuceria. Soon most of the seats were occupied and there was a mass of red and blue in the amphitheatre worn or carried by supporters.

As the time for the games to start drew near, a band of musicians began to play, adding an air of occasion to the scene. Colourful and amusing acrobats also entered the stadium, their performances adding colour and a sense of frivolity.

Farzana and Aeneus reached the first of the drink kiosks set up in the shade between the umbrella pines near the entry to the stadium. Farzana laughed at the spruiking going on between the sellers.

'Would you like a cool drink?' Aeneus offered.

'That would be lovely.'

He bought two cups of cold lemon drink, and took her elbow to help her through the crowd. Farzana looked up at the double stairs that led to the top of the arena.

'No. Not up there!' Aeneus shook his head as he steered her away from the stairs. 'Custom is a little more relaxed here than in Rome. We'll sit together about half-way up,' he explained. 'I'm not going to leave you right at the top on your own. Anyone who doesn't like it can take it up with me.' That would be unlikely to happen, Farzana knew, as he was wearing his uniform. She concluded that how he was dressed was probably not an accident.

It had the effect of building her sense of safety and security. She was really beginning to enjoy herself. She liked the warm, fuzzy feeling of having someone to look after her. For once she wasn't alone, or perhaps, with her brother. They settled in to watch the entertainment.

Farzana would say later, that what happened that afternoon passed by in a blur. First, was an uninspiring bout between an inexperienced Thracian from Nuceria and a huge, mountain of a man, a Murmillo fighting for Pompeii. The crowd yawned and talked amongst themselves, bored and not too worried about the result which was a win for the Thracian. The next bout was a very different matter. Although it was not "to the death," which rarely happened in Pompeii, it was a matter of pride.

Jucundus, the wealthy banker and patron of the games looked on importantly. Holding these games was one of the ways in which he displayed his apparent generosity to the citizens.

Two experienced and skilled gladiators faced one another. The Retiarius entered to the cheers of those in the crowd from Pompeii, while the Nucerians gave a rousing reception to his Secutor opponent.

The rudis stood between them. Moments later the bout was underway. *Remember to concentrate,* the Secutor reminded himself, as the Retiarius made a feint towards him with his net. They circled around stalking each other, and looking for an advantage.

'Fight, you coward!' yelled one of the Nucerians in the crowd. 'The Pompeians, they're all spineless!'

Defensively, the gladiators continued circling, as each man watched the eyes of his opponent for any hint of his next move. It was quickly apparent from the way he moved that the Secutor was slow.

Personally, Aeneus didn't really care too much which of the gladiators won the bout, but he was amused to see how involved Farzana became, rising from her seat and shouting.

As the Secutor lunged towards him, the Retiarius managed to entangle him with his net. His opponent was disadvantaged being unable to see in front of himself except through two tiny eye holes in his helmet. He fell to the ground, struggling frantically to escape.

The Retiarius stood over his opponent as his own supporters threw red roses down onto the sand of the arena, yelling in triumph. Jucundus indicated to the referee that he should stop the fight.

As the gladiators left the arena, some in the crowd became aware that two men in the crowd had begun brawling. It didn't take long before more joined in. The fight quickly began to spread, reaching closer to where Aeneus and Farzana were sitting.

He took her firmly by the arm and propelled her towards the exit. They were fortunate to have left early enough to avoid the major stampede to get out.

'I need your horse!' Aeneus yelled to one of the praetorians on horseback outside. The praetorian's response was immediate. Urgently, Aeneus mounted up with Farzana behind him. 'Put your arms around me and hold on tight,' he yelled.

It seemed like only a few minutes until she was home again with Aulus, surprised, opening the door to the pounding on it. 'What's happened?'

'I have to get back to the stadium, I've got a feeling I'm going to be needed,' Aeneus shouted without saying more, as he turned his horse and rode back towards the arena.

The fighting went on for what seemed like an age. Only a few praetorians were on duty that day as no trouble had been anticipated. Women in the crowd fled through the archways out of the arena, searching for safety. Most of the men stayed to fight as years of hostile competition between the two cities finally flared to fever pitch.

The crowd riot at the gladiator games that day was the worst ever seen in Pompeii, or Rome, for that matter. Reports suggested that the Pompeii supporters won the battle. Even so, many of them were injured. Many more of those from Nuceria were also injured some more seriously.

No one seemed sure which side had started it all.

News of the riot reached Nero who was furious. He decreed that no more bouts would be held in Pompeii for a decade. Pompeians were incensed. They argued with the Duumvir of the city that they hadn't started the fight so why should they be punished? Poppy's concern was for Farzana. Had she been at the arena and if so, was she safe?

Poppy dispatched an urgent message to her;

Dearest Farzana,

I've just received news of the riot there. Please let me know that you are safe. I'm worried about you. I'll write again soon but for now I'm sending this to you urgently.

Love,
Poppy

Daughter of Pompeii

After some time had passed, Poppy interceded with Nero and the games were allowed to recommence. She didn't quite understand why he was so angry about it, but had to admit to herself, that she hadn't been there, nor had she read the reports that reached the palace from Rome. For Pompeii, it was a day of rioting that would be passed down in history.

There were more outings and Farzana and Aeneus grew ever closer. Her father accepted him gladly and they often spent time together playing dice.

One morning Aeneus appeared at the door and asked to speak with Farzana alone. They stepped outside the house and then he held her close.

'I'm sorry, Farzana, but I've been posted to Rome. I leave in a few days. I'll never forget you and if you'll wait, I'll come back for you.'

Farzana didn't know what to say. She had tears in her eyes. She wasn't foolish enough to think that this man who was, she believed, ready to marry, would not become entranced with someone else in Rome. He'd quickly forget her.

'I understand, Aeneus,' she managed to say. 'We've had a wonderful time together and I hope that life is good to you.'

They parted as friends and she cried herself to sleep that night. She'd thought all along that their friendship seemed too good to be true, but that didn't heal her grieving heart.

Aulus was disappointed.

He really liked Aeneus and felt very comfortable at the thought of having him around, perhaps, permanently. He didn't see as much of Marcellus now, as he always seemed to be working on some project or other dreamed up by his wife for their house.

Aulus particularly missed having Aeneus play dice, knuckle bones or some other game against him where they could laugh together, have a cup or two of wine, and the evenings would pass in pleasant companionship. It seemed that fate had separated the two young people.

Although Farzana tried to hid her misery, Aulus was well aware of just how upset she was and how much she missed Aeneus. He just couldn't think of a way to cheer her up. He spent many afternoons just walking in the sunshine trying to think of how he could make things better, but the remedy remained elusive for a problem that he just couldn't solve.

15

BAIAE

Nero's Villa

It was at Baiae that Nero decided to kill his mother.

As he stared out from his balcony across the bay towards Misenum, he imagined Agrippina scheming and plotting his downfall in her country estate. He was sick and tired of her insatiable lust for power, and he knew that there was no way she'd simply stay away from the action for long. Then she'd be back.

He told Poppy in a matter of fact tone of voice one day after breakfast. She felt a cold shiver run down her spine, but kept her voice carefully neutral.

'I see. Well, perhaps we should get rid of Octavia as well,' Poppy responded.

'Is that really necessary?'

'Of course, it's necessary.' Poppy assured him calmly. 'You would like me to be your empress, surely.'

'You know I would, but we have to get the timing right.'

'The earlier you do it the better,' Poppy pressed her case, 'and that's not nearly such an issue as whether you should kill Agrippina.'

'No. But Octavia has done nothing wrong.' Nero held up his hand to indicate that the subject was closed, at least for the moment.

Poppy was elated. If Nero would kill his mother, she rationalised, then killing Octavia shouldn't be too much of a problem for him. For the time being, she'd wait and watch.

'Tigellinus, I need you to arrange something for me,' Nero told him when he entered the villa the next day. I want you to engage the best boat builders you can find, to build a small boat that can be made to fall apart once well out into the bay.'

'Fall apart?' Tigellinus echoed, incredulous.

'Yes. I think I've found a way to get rid of my mother.'

'Agrippina?' the praetorian commander's face showed his amazement.

'Stop repeating everything I say,' Nero ordered irritably. 'I need this done as soon as possible. I shall invite her to dinner here but when she leaves Misenum the boat will fall apart and she'll drown.'

'I'll have to pay the men well who do this so they keep their mouths shut,' Tigellinus warned.

'I don't have a problem with that, but they need to understand that the only other option is that they'll be murdered on a dark night somewhere. That warning should keep them quiet.'

Misenum

Agrippina liked the early morning and the sight of the sun as it fled the night to bring life again to the earth. By day Misenum could also look harsh as bright sunlight struck the port and naval structures that provided both protection and practical support for the Roman fleet.

Since her exile she'd quite enjoyed the peace and quiet of her estate and a rest from the political affairs that had eddied and flowed around her in Rome. But Agrippina was becoming restless and beginning to plot her return. It was true that she couldn't stay away from interfering in the political happenings of the day.

'A message has arrived for you, Domina.'

'Tell the messenger to wait.'

Agrippina opened the message, quickly scanning it. A look of sheer satisfaction spread slowly across her face.

She'd won! Everything was going to be all right after all.

Nero couldn't manage without her. Agrippina had been sure that he'd recall her. She re-read the message from him:

> *Would she have dinner with him at his villa in Baiae? He'd be pleased to send a boat to transport her there, then home again. He was looking forward to seeing her.*

Agrippina wondered what she should wear and immediately called her maid to assist her with a choice. She couldn't dress in black, that would be too serious. Soon her clothes were spread out over her bed and on top of every available space.

She was determined to sparkle with her conversation and also her appearance. She would charm her son again the way she used to when he was young. Their row had just been a mistake she was sure. She wrote a formal acceptance and called for the messenger.

'She's accepted!' Nero told Poppy with glee as he read Agrippina's reply. 'I must meet with Tigellinus and make sure that nothing goes wrong. If it does, she'll know she's been tricked and then there will be chaos the like of which Rome has never seen.'

'I'm going for a walk. I'll be back in time for dinner,' Poppy told him. She picked up a shawl from where it lay across a chair, just in case it became cool. Nero was so involved in his own plans that he barely grunted in reply.

Poppy went down to the sandy beach and walked along it towards the theatre, the same way she'd walked before on her first visit with Otho. So much seemed to have happened since then that it hardly seemed possible.

So much had changed. She had changed.

She sat down on the solitary beach where the sand met the grass. For the first time she questioned where life was leading her. Everything had moved too fast. And Nero had mentally deteriorated, his ideas and demands becoming more extreme. Whichever way Poppy looked at it, she felt as if she was on a path that couldn't be altered now even if she wanted to.

As to murdering Agrippina she was stunned. She hated the woman and found her aggressive and ambitious for ultimate power, but she was Nero's mother. It seemed unnatural, but it was not her decision to make.

She thought of her own mother, so loved and missed. How she wished she could just talk to her or hear her voice. She was also missing Farzana, which didn't surprise her. She'd write to her and see if she could find out when she was coming back from Pompeii.

Poppy decided that she would have no qualms about getting rid of Octavia, though. She had to look after herself which meant achieving more power. Otherwise, she'd become another Acte. Sometimes, in her dreams, she saw her again, and imagined her crying for the life she'd lost. There was no way Poppy wanted that to happen to her, so she was always vigilant.

On the night planned for her death Agrippina strode confidently down to the water and seated herself comfortably in the boat that was waiting for her. It was a clear, warm night and the sea was as clear and calm as glass. There wasn't even a hint of a breeze. She was actually looking forward to the short trip across the water.

'You may begin,' she ordered the two crewmen.

'Yes, Domina.'

When half-way through the journey, they pulled pieces from the structure as instructed. Soon, the boat began to list to one side. Agrippina called to them to find out what was happening. They reassured her, telling her that it seemed unlikely there would be a problem given the calmness of the sea.

'Domina, I'm sure there will be no need to worry. The boat is new so it shouldn't sink.'

But slowly, it began to collapse.

As it fell further and further below the surface, Agrippina decided to swim. She struck out for the shoreline, unaware that Nero's hidden watchers, having seen that she was likely to save herself, sent urgently to him asking what to do. Fearing that she'd live and know that he'd planned her death, Nero took immediate action-he spoke to Seneca in a panic.

'What should I do?' he was far from calm enough to act to his best advantage.

Seneca paused, then made his decision.

'Get someone to kill her, of course. Just make sure they do it *now* before any news of this gets out!'

Anicetus, commander of the Roman Fleet at Misenum but presently staying at his villa at Baiae, was advised of the situation by a praetorian, travelling in great urgency.

'By order of the Emperor,' the praetorian advised him, 'Agrippina must not live!'

As she was brought to Anicetus' door seeking safety, he drew his gladius and stabbed her. A message was immediately sent to Nero advising him and the next morning he came to see her body.

He examined it slowly and methodically pronouncing that he hadn't realised that he had such a beautiful mother. Anicetus, who was standing beside him, was horrified.

From that day onwards, Nero suffered from terrible nightmares during which ghosts holding flaming torches chased him as he ran for his life:

> *You killed me. You killed your own mother!*
> *You made me do it with your incessant push for power.*
> *But, to kill your own mother? What sort of a man does that?*

Nero and Poppy returned to Rome. He woke each day covered in sweat and exhausted, with Agrippina's voice always ringing in his head.

Poppy tried in vain to help him. Nero's sanity hung by a thread.

16

ROME

The Royal Palace
Two Weeks Later

Octavia's beauty was subtle. The reflection that met her anxious glance in the mirror showed a woman, still young, with brown hair and blue eyes. She was slight in build and of medium height. She'd promised herself time after time that she'd stop comparing herself to Nero's mistress in the mirror, but she didn't seem to be able to help herself. Her delicate beauty looked washed out beside Poppy's flaming hair and green eyes.

Her mind went back to the gladiator bouts several days before. She'd dropped her shawl when leaving and it was picked up and held out to her by a young praetorian. She'd looked into his grey eyes and smiled at him. It was a surprisingly intimate moment for one so fleeting. There was something kind about his glance at her.

'Dreaming again!' Octavia chided herself. She would remain chained to Nero whether she like it or not. It wasn't much of a life but there was also nothing she could do about it.

'Domina, I bear a message from the Emperor.' Her maid entered the room and handed the parchment to Octavia.

Nero requested an audience with her that afternoon. He would come alone as he had something important to say to her.

'Alia, please send a messenger to tell Caesar that his wish is my command.'

After her maid had gone Octavia found it difficult to apply herself to anything. Nero never came to her apartment so she wondered what could be so important. By the time he arrived, her nerves were taut. He sauntered into the room, his face stern and his expression unbending as he looked around him.

'Octavia, ever the good empress,' he remarked sarcastically as he noticed a Bona Dea document on her desk. 'You're such a hard worker for charity, aren't you?' he sneered. 'Well, I'm afraid from now on they're going to have to do without you.'

Octavia stood to face him, her chin lifted and her head held high. She knew now that this was no pleasant encounter, but even though Nero showed her no respect, she was an empress and would retain her dignity.

'I'll keep this short,' he snapped. 'It's unfortunate for you that Agrippina is no longer here so that you can run to her for help! I'm divorcing you. You'll be sent into exile somewhere with a sweet little house and garden.'

'I wondered how long it would take before you decided to get me out of the way,' Octavia said evenly. 'Who asked you to do this, was it your mistress?'

Nero snarled at her. 'I make my own decisions, this is nothing to do with her.'

At first Octavia thought he would strike her, but then he moved away from her closer to the door. She stared at him with reproach.

'You'll leave in two days with praetorians to guard you. I'm sure you'll be happier somewhere that doesn't require you to handle affairs of state. You're too insipid for that. Goodbye, Octavia. I doubt that we'll meet again.'

Nero spun on his heel and left without another word.

It didn't take long for the gossip to spread. How the news leaked from the palace no one ever knew, but the people did know that Octavia had been sent into exile.

I wonder what's going on at court?
Where's she been sent?
Why did Nero do it?

All of these questions and more circulated throughout the city and spread to nearby towns. In Rome, people stood around bars or sat drinking at tables on the footpath as they talked and spread rumours. One thing that became clear, was that the plebs had no intention of their beloved empress being treated in such a manner. They gathered in public bathhouses and in smaller groups in insulae to discuss the problem.

Before long they took matters into their own hands. Huge crowds gathered in the Forum and elsewhere, carrying statues of Octavia which they garlanded with flowers then paraded through the streets. Violence began to break out.

Statues of Nero were torn down and burned and the mob began to torch public buildings.

The people demanded the return of their empress.

When it became obvious that there would not be an end to the demonstrations, Nero called Tigellinus to a meeting to discuss the situation.

'Can't you force them to go home?' he complained petulantly. 'Don't they have more to do with their time than this?'

'I'm sorry to say that there are far too many of them, Caesar,' was Tigellinus' reply. 'But, if some solution isn't found soon, I fear that there will be an increase in bloodshed.'

'What do you suggest?' Nero queried as he slouched lower down in his chair.

'A simple solution, Caesar. Bring Octavia back!'

'You must be joking!' Nero got up suddenly and began pacing the room. 'Give in to their demands?'

'Do you have any other course of action that will work?' the praetorian prefect retorted.

'Do it quickly, then,' Nero snapped. 'Before they burn down the city and make sure you severely punish those who started this.'

Nero dispatched an urgent message to Campania as Tigellinus hurried from the palace. His guards were having trouble controlling the masses, but at least he'd been able to convince Nero to give the order. He expected the situation to revert to normal once the guards retaliated.

It took some time for word of Octavia's imminent return to flow through to the crowds, before which there was open fighting in the Forum and the area around the Campus Martius. Finally, the announcement coupled with the physical mastery by the guards sent the mob, bloodied and angry, back to their homes and places of employment.

Poppy was furious! She'd been so close to achieving her goal only to have it blow up in her face. She seethed with anger but knew better than to question Nero's decision. Sweet little Octavia, already in Campania, would soon be back at court. It was a disaster.

Poppy suddenly reached a decision. She'd write to Farzana, the most level-headed, sensible person she knew. Poppy would put the question of what to do for the best to her, and see what she replied. Calling for parchment and a stylus she set to work.

The answer when she received it was so far from anything she'd expected, that she felt she needed to sit down:

Dearest Poppy,

I feel for you in this situation with Octavia. Remember, sometimes you must try more than once to get what you want! If Octavia comes back you should act immediately, otherwise she'll remain permanently. I suggest that you must be brave enough to risk everything.

Try to get Nero to reverse his decision. If he refuses tell him you will leave him!

There is no other way if you really want to become Empress. Let me know what comes of it. I wish you luck.

I miss you but have not yet made up my mind whether to leave my family and return to Rome. It's not an easy decision.

Love

Farzana

By the time Octavia arrived back in Rome, Poppy's adrenaline level had well and truly risen and was pumping through her as she prepared for a confrontation with Nero. She chose to speak to him soon after the protests had calmed and everything appeared to be back to normal.

'How long is Octavia staying back in Rome?' she asked casually as he read one of the poems he'd written and eaten his favourite meal.

'She's back and that's that!'

'No. That's not that!'

'What are you talking about?' he glanced at her sharply.

'What it's about is that I want her sent back into exile.'

'Why?'

'Let us not play games, you know why.'

'I won't do it!' Nero glared at her. 'It's far too disruptive. You saw what's just happened.'

'If that's your final decision, then I will leave you!' Poppy's heart thumped in her chest as she pushed for all or nothing. She'd win-or- lose the lot.

Shocked, Nero was speechless. He stared at her in disbelief, frozen.

'Please retire. You'll have my decision tomorrow.'

Poppy left the room hoping that everything she'd worked for wasn't lost.

17

Poppy was sitting in her apartment trying to look unconcerned when Nero was announced the next morning. She stood to receive him, a welcome smile on her face, but feeling decidedly nauseous.

'Leave us!' he ordered her ladies and they fled the room.

He moved swiftly to take her in his arms. 'You are my greatest treasure,' he murmured, 'and I cannot risk losing you.'

'You will divorce Octavia?'

'Yes. Then, we can marry.'

'Thank you,' she breathed.

'If it is your wish then it will be so. The arrangements will be made immediately. Now, I must leave you to take care of the necessary steps to arrange it.'

Nero hurried out of the room leaving Poppy able to relax once more. Her thoughts went to Farzana. Her friend had been right. She must reward her well for her loyalty and counsel.

Octavia received the official notice of her impending exile by messenger. The charge against her was adultery and also being barren. Surely, that was a joke! She barely knew the man she was supposed to have seduced. As to the second charge, Nero never came near her so it wasn't surprising that there had been no children born.

She sighed. She hadn't even had the respect of a personal notification. Her reprieve had been short and this time she knew there would be no saving her.

'Alia, you will be packing for me to leave. You won't have much time. Call for help from the other maids or you'll never finish in time. I'm not taking everything but even so, I'll need the essentials.'

'But, Domina, you've only just returned,' Alia stated the obvious.

'I know, but I have no choice.'

Octavia began to gather together the possessions that she really valued. There were several small gifts, a couple of favourite pieces of clothing and a few pieces of jewellery. She couldn't imagine why she bothered with the latter, except that they reminded her of better times.

On the day she was due to leave Rome, she woke very early and as the sun came up she walked by the Tiber. The river's currents were strong and she wondered whether she should end everything now, before it was forced upon her, but found that she didn't have the courage.

The Theatre of Marcellus stood strong and reassuring by the riverbank and she wandered through to the Forum where she entered one of the temples. When she'd finished praying for acceptance, she stood on the hill above the curia and looked across the Forum and up to the Palatine, trying to imprint on her memory the city she loved so dearly. She wanted to always be able to remember how it looked at this moment, so that it would remain with her forever.

Daughter of Pompeii

As the first blush of dawn began to turn into daylight, she walked slowly to the palace. Wearily she made her way back to her rooms to check that her belongings were packed and ready.

Octavia was sitting by the window looking out onto the gardens when the guards came for her. She stood as they entered. The senior praetorian addressed her.

'Are you ready to leave? I can give you a few minutes if that would assist you.'

Octavia turned and looked up at him. She saw that it was the same guard who had retrieved her shawl at the games. His grey eyes held a look of concern.

'Thank you for offering, but I believe my time here is over.'

She knew that she'd never see Rome again and it broke her heart. She'd been proud to be empress to its people.

'Where are you taking me?' Octavia asked as they left the palace, 'at least it can do no harm to tell me my destination.'

'Our orders, lady, are to take you to the island of Pandataria and leave you there.' The praetorian's face was grim.

Octavia shuddered.

'You will be given one servant to attend you during your stay,' he continued.

Octavia was silent. So, exile to the notorious island from which very few ever returned was to be her fate. She felt tears in her eyes spill down her cheeks, and knew that there would be no appeal and no escape from the hell to which Nero had sentenced her. He was truly a monster.

Poppy watched on, unseen, as Octavia and her entourage left the palace. She resolved to feel no sympathy for her. Surely, if their roles had been reversed, Octavia would not have considered Poppy's welfare, at least, that's what she persuaded herself, pushing aside the persistent niggle within her that told her otherwise.

She stood by the window for some time after Octavia's departure. Then, banishing it from her thoughts, she returned to thinking about the plans that she'd need to make for the spectacular ceremonies that would declare her ascent to the throne. The very thought of it thrilled and delighted her.

This was her moment and hers alone.

The Island of Pandataria
(Ventotene)

Octavia stood huddled into her shawl attempting to subdue the cold that seeped into her bones from the wind that was chopping up the waves. She found it ironical that the island's outline she could just see ahead of them, lay directly in a line from the Roman coastal party town of Baiae. Pandataria was, however, many miles out to sea.

The boat made its way towards a bay on the island with a thin strip of sandy beach. Its terrain was rocky with a mountainous interior. A long, steep trek took the small party up to the palace.

Octavia's first observation was that no one had obviously worried much about maintenance. Inside, were a number of quite spacious rooms but they were sparsely furnished. The wall frescoes were faded and chipped and some of the floor mosaic tesserae were broken.

Closest to the water's edge was a bathhouse. It had been built many years before and long battered by the sea. It was still very usable, however, and had originally been very luxurious.

Food stores were carried from the boat by the guards to supplement the meagre supplies in the kitchen. It was obvious that she would have the barest minimum necessary for survival.

'This is your servant, she lives in a small hut on the island,' the senior praetorian informed Octavia as he introduced a middle-aged woman with greasy hair who stood before her surly and silent.

It was obvious that the slave wasn't there to provide company. Octavia wondered what the woman's duties were supposed to be and if, perhaps, she was a spy.

'We'll leave you now. A boat will bring you food from time to time. Salve.'

Octavia sat down feeling baffled as to why she was even on this island. She saw herself as no threat to anyone in Rome's power elite. There was, however, Poppy. She'd been no friend to Octavia and seemed the natural culprit who'd benefit, but she couldn't bring herself to believe that even ambitious as she knew Poppy to be, she'd been responsible for this.

The ridiculous part of this whole situation, as far as Octavia was concerned, was that Nero had only to ask her and she'd have stepped down willingly, even gratefully, from her status as empress. It could have been done very quietly and she'd have disappeared from sight to live a comfortable but unremarkable life somewhere of her choice.

Nero's confidence was so low, however, that he'd never have allowed it. And so, she must die.

Already, Octavia felt desperately lonely.

'May the gods protect you,' Sextus, the senior praetorian told her as his grey eyes looked into hers and he turned away, the last to leave. The guards departed, leaving her robbed of all hope.

Octavia was grateful that she'd remembered to include writing materials in the items she'd brought with her. Perhaps she'd write her story. There was no one to interrupt her. Pouring herself a cup of the mediocre wine supplied for her use, she began to write:

> "I wondered why everyone around me was whispering. But I was only a young child and did not understand. The Emperor, Claudius, had just ordered the execution of my mother......."

Eventually, Octavia tired of writing and put down the stylus. She'd had several cups of wine by then and felt both a little drowsy as well as dizzy. She glanced out towards the sea, noticing once again the bathing area out in the open, right beside the water.

It looked inviting and the day was still warm now that the wind had dropped. Somewhat unsteadily, she got up and walked through the room out towards the circular bathing pool, its floor lined with blue and green tesserae. And then she did something that completely reversed everything she'd ever done before.

Octavia totally stripped off all of her clothing and entered the pool. It felt like pure luxury and she sighed with delight. How long she sat and frolicked alone there with no one to see her she didn't know and didn't care.

In that short time of complete and utter freedom, unimpeded by the expectations and rules of others and someone's eyes always watching her, she found a part of herself that she'd had no idea existed. Her only regret, was that she hadn't found it earlier.

18

After their return to Rome from Baiae, Poppy didn't particularly like the idea of an unstable husband trailing around the palace after her, or taking part in weird activities. After much thought she decided that part of the remedy for Nero would be entering into more of the pursuits he really enjoyed. She raised the subject a few days later over dinner.

'I hear there's a music festival being held in Napoli soon. Have you thought about performing there?' she asked.

Nero looked up at her, suddenly alert.

'Do you think that I should?'

'Why not? You haven't been paying much attention to your music lately. Why don't you send for Terpnus and he can teach you again?'

'What a wonderful idea!' Nero jumped up from the couch, excited. 'I can play my lyre, that would certainly be a special treat for the people. They don't all have the opportunity to hear me play and sing if I only perform in Rome.'

Nero returned to his singing exercises and practising the lyre, and his mood improved with every day. In return for Poppy's wonderful suggestion, he came to visit her several days later in her apartment.

'I have a thank you gift. It's also an early wedding gift for you, but you'll have to leave Rome to see it,' he whispered in her ear. Poppy's face broke out in a smile and she embraced him impulsively

'I can't believe it,' she exclaimed. 'How very generous you are!'

Nero was delighted to see her so excited.

After he'd left her apartment, Poppy sat down to write a message to Farzana to tell her that she'd arrive in Pompeii very soon, as she was leaving Rome immediately.

Terpnus turned up promptly to the palace to work with Nero. He went back onto his old training diet and physical exercises and was ordered not to eat apples, as they were not good for his voice.

Poppy disliked the man. He was fawning and had a face like a ferret, but she didn't care as long as he kept Nero happy. Poppy could hear Terpnus encouraging and trying to inspire his pupil. It sounded as if it was hard work, but he was being paid a small fortune to do it.

The sound of the lyre and singing could be heard floating from Nero's apartment during the day. His voice was pleasant enough, but had little strength in it. As for the lyre, he was competent in his playing of the instrument but that was all. By night, Nero performed for those invited to hear him at the palace and his excitement grew as they applauded him and the music festival drew ever nearer.

Pompeii

Poppy wasted no time in departing the palace. She was plainly dressed. After a night's sleep in Napoli at a villa belonging to one of Rome's senators, she resumed her journey. The day was mild and the countryside quiet. She glanced up at the vine-covered mountain that loomed over Pompeii, paying little heed to it, and before long her carriage clattered through the Herculaneum Gate.

'Please stop for a few moments.'

She stepped down and walked the small distance to her mother's mausoleum. It seemed to her to be so long ago that she'd said goodbye to her. The pain she felt was still very deep.

Poppy had kept her promise to avenge her mother. Soon, she'd be Empress of Rome.

I hope you're proud of me. I've achieved our revenge.

Returning to the carriage, she travelled the short distance to Farzana's house on Via Consolare. Time rolled backwards for her as in her mind, she relived her first visit.

'Poppy! Is it really you?'

Farzana came rushing to greet her and the two women embraced. A couple of passers-by glanced at them curiously but were unaware of the visitor's identity and soon looked away. Nero had wanted her to have a few praetorians travel with her but Poppy had insisted on only one. If there were any problems, she would call for help from the Nucerian praetorian barracks.

'May I still call you Poppy?' Aulus asked as he came to welcome her.

'That is who I'll always be to your family,' Poppy replied, laughing. 'Where is Marcellus?'

'He's married now,' Farzana told her. 'We thought you'd prefer it if we kept this visit very quiet. He'll slip away and come over later to join us if it's possible. Even his wife doesn't know about your visit.'

They entered the small front room where Poppy had bought sandals from Aulus so many years before.

Poppy turned to look at him. 'Aulus, I have to tell you that I wore those sandals for years, and they were admired by so many in Rome who saw them.'

Aulus beamed with pleasure. 'They were beautiful sandals for a beautiful young woman,' he complimented her.

They talked together for some time then Poppy turned to Farzana. 'How do you feel about taking a walk to the Temple of Venus with me. We could sit and talk in the garden as we did so long ago?'

'I agree,' she answered, 'it would be so good to go back there again together.'

Arm in arm they strolled to the temple and sat on the same stone seat that was still there. The fragrance of roses reached them on a slight breeze.

Farzana told Poppy all about Aeneus. Then, she listened as Poppy related the many things that had happened to her in Rome.

'I have a proposition to put to you,' she whispered to Farzana, but soon I'll have to go. I'm sorry but I'll miss seeing Marcellus this time.'

As the morning passed and the heat grew, Poppy gave a key and a purse full of gold coins to Farzana as she returned to her carriage.

19

The Villa of Oplontis
(Outside Pompeii)

Poppy peered from the carriage as it approached the villa's sentry box. It was empty. A newly built brick wall restricted entry, although the heavy gates stood open. The wall's bareness was softened by the overhanging branches of a lush mulberry tree. On seeing the carriage's royal emblem, an approaching guard waved her through to the front of the villa.

Poppy stepped down.

Her senses were immediately assaulted by the multitude of colours, sounds and perfumes surrounding her. She turned her back on the villa entrance and instead, walked slowly into the garden.

'So, this is what it means to be desired by an emperor,' she whispered to herself as she gazed at the manicured box hedges, violets, marigolds, gladioli and poppies around her. She finally had what she wanted. This was Nero's gift to her for their marriage. She would be Empress of Rome.

Looking around her eyes widened in disbelief as she studied the enormous swimming pool, the largest she'd ever seen. This place was almost too stunning to be believed.

Poppy made her way along a gravel pathway that led towards the sea. The villa was perched on top of a cliff overlooking the surging waves that thundered onto the rocks below, flinging white plumes of water into the air. She found the power of the sea both enticing and disturbing. An unwanted chill of fear ran through her and she turned away trying to free herself from a momentary flash of indecision. Poppy shook it off. It was time to see the inside of the villa. She was totally unprepared for the panorama that met her eyes as she walked inside through a door beyond the pool. Entering the atrium, she caught her breath with wonder.

Her own family's villa in Pompeii was wealthy, but this was something on a much grander, more impressive scale. Richly coloured frescoes filled the walls contrasting with the white floor mosaic. She walked further through the interior into the major part of the villa including the private bath area.

Looking up in one of the rooms Poppy found herself being scrutinised by a gaudily painted peacock, its arrogant eyes fastened on her. From the villa's shaded colonnades to the magnificence of the interior with its rich red, blue and gold frescoed walls filled with plants and birds, the villa was pure opulence.

She stood gazing for some time at the private indoor garden that mimicked what lay in the garden outside, but this was far more intimate. Here, was everything she'd ever dreamed of except it was far more sumptuous.

Free from prying eyes Poppy threw her head back with a laugh of sheer triumph then pirouetted across the broad expanse of the cool marble floor. She danced until it made her head spin. And, this was only the beginning. She defied the gods to convince her otherwise.

But the gods would not be mocked. Outside the villa, storm clouds rolled in from the sea, but for once, Poppy's usual strong instinct for survival in the face of approaching danger deserted her. Eventually, as the rain fell, she re-entered her carriage and continued on to Rome.

Farzana, with the key Poppy had given her, would become the part time live-in caretaker of the villa and employ the necessary staff to ensure that it remained safe. The remainder of the time, she'd live with her family in Pompeii.

When she returned to Rome, Poppy would order furnishings and everything else necessary so that the villa became once more a place of utter comfort. Fresco painters and mosaic builders as well as sculptors, gardeners and other workers would be paid to beautify the building and grounds. And as often as she could, Poppy would live in the villa with Farzana enjoying the extravagant life she'd worked so hard to attain.

Poppy was surprised to realise that she was tired of Rome. There was very little real privacy and the constant dinners and parties no longer excited her.

In Oplontis she'd find peace and contentment.

A couple of days later, Farzana visited Poppy's villa. She was astounded at its beauty and knew that she'd enjoy taking responsibility for its welfare. She'd love living in the villa from time to time especially if Poppy was there.

What Poppy didn't tell Farzana was that she'd have a quiet word in the ear of Tigellinus. 'There is in Rome a certain praetorian trooper by the name of Aeneus Capito. Could you, Tigellinus, find it in your heart as a favour to me, to transfer him back to the barracks at Nuceria?'

Poppy informed him that she had a strong feeling there would be some favour in the form of cash or land that she might provide for him in return.

Rome

Aeneus sat drinking with a few friends in one of the better bars at the edge of the Forum. As he enjoyed his wine he watched one of Rome's less presentable citizens scrawling a lewd cartoon featuring Nero on an outside wall. That wasn't an unusual pastime for many of the common people, but was usually done at night when no one was able to identify the culprit.

He grinned as he saw a praetorian approaching. *Now he's for it!* he thought, but was surprised to see the guard walk on, simply glaring at the man then heading straight for the bar. He walked up to Aeneus' table looking hopeful.

'Are you trooper Capito?'

'Yes,' Aeneus replied with an expression of bewilderment.

The messenger looked relieved. 'Thanks to the gods! I didn't fancy walking into every bar in the neighbourhood trying to find you. I've been sent to order your immediate return to Nuceria.'

Surprised, Aeneus was escorted back to the Castra Praetoria and given written orders. He'd tried to find out more information from the messenger on the way, but he said he knew nothing further, except there had been rumours that Aeneus had been promoted.

Aeneus found himself out of Rome quicker than he could drink a beaker of wine. Come to think of it, he'd only half-finished the one he'd been drinking at the bar. He was not unhappy about returning to Nuceria, the only problem being that there wasn't much to do for entertainment. There was, however, one very genuine reason that he was happy to be back.

'I came as quickly as I could after I arrived,' Aeneus explained to Farzana a couple of days later as she opened the door to his knock. 'For some reason, I've been transferred back to Nuceria, but I've also been given a promotion! I'm so happy to see you again, I've missed you.' He hugged her tightly.

Farzana was speechless, then ecstatic. They planned to meet again the next day and take a walk over to watch the throwing competition at the palestra.

As she lay awake that night thinking about the events of the day, especially with Aeneus being back, she began to laugh. She suddenly realised that this was Poppy's work, of course. And she was grateful.

'What's so funny?' Aulus asked as he walked past her door.

'Apart from genuine friendship, there is definitely something to be said for being the best friend of the Empress of Rome,' she explained, 'but you wouldn't understand.'

Aulus shook his head wisely and walked on, pleased that Farzana was happy again. Tigellinus was even more happy. He became the owner of a small parcel of fertile land near Cumae.

Aeneus knew he was falling in love with Farzana. She was pretty and the companion he felt he'd like to spend his life with. He'd been in the Guard for some years and felt that a change might also be right for him now. The problem was that if he married he'd have to leave the Guard. He had absolutely no idea of what he would do in terms of finding employment.

The barracks in Nuceria wasn't far at all from Pompeii. As a praetorian barracks it was a small but quite a solid, fortified building that was comfortable and where decent food was served. It was a pleasant life, but Aeneus resolved that he'd speak to Farzana about his intentions next time they met.

Whether she'd wait to marry him until he'd saved enough so they could live comfortably was uppermost in his mind. The promotion he'd just received might just make that possible. Without that, it would have been a long wait. It occurred to him as a little strange that he'd been sent to Rome then posted straight back to Nuceria. What he'd done to earn a promotion he also had no idea.

Aeneus thought, overall, that his unusual situation seemed to be a positive one though. All he had to do was to persuade Farzana to marry him.

20

Napoli
(Naples)

Excitement rose to fever pitch as Nero and his mounted praetorian guards approached the city of Napoli under a pitiless, blue sky. Terpnus sat beside him looking edgy and not quite sure what to expect.

He knew that it was reasonable for Nero to demand that his attendance should be part of his duties. After all, it wasn't unusual to want him to be there when his pupil performed, especially as he was Emperor of Rome.

Terpnus couldn't help wishing, though, that he was anywhere else but sitting in this carriage. If it was attacked, there was a chance he'd also be killed.

Terpnus was not a brave man.

'This is a magnificent welcome, don't you think?'

'It certainly is, Caesar,' Terpnus struggled to reply.

Crowds lined his way cheering as they tried to catch a glimpse of their emperor. Nero smiled and waved graciously as the praetorians attempted to hold back those who crushed in upon them in their fervour. It was a colourful, noise-filled scene full of goodwill. Fathers held their children up so they could see and many of the women scattered flower petals before him.

Nero could see Tigellinus nearest to him helping to protect the carriage. As long as he had the backing of the praetorian commander and his guards, he knew he could feel secure whether he was here or in Rome.

The city forum when they reached it, was an echo of the great Forum in Rome and although so much smaller, Nero was pleased to see the same activities being enacted there.

They passed slowly through the narrow streets, grimy with the passage of time, as people hung half out of their apartment windows for a look at the Emperor and his entourage. Some of them held up symbols of luck to greet Nero, red, gold or silver horns, or others in the shape of a hand or a phallus.

Finally, they reached the other side of the city where the crowd had thinned. This city was very much a place with a very Greek feeling and heritage.

They made their way toward the best villa in Napoli, owned by one of the city's wealthiest families. Nero was pleased to see that it seemed to have every amenity he could wish for as well as a magnificent view of the bay, famed for its beauty.

He was a little disappointed that Poppy wasn't with him but she'd made the point that he needed to be seen as powerful and independent, relying on no one else. Also, she had much to do, considering that their marriage and her coronation as empress would be held soon.

The next morning was set aside for practice at the theatre which was close to the forum. All of the contestants appeared on stage one by one to play or sing as practice for that afternoon's performance. Nero could feel his anxiety level rising.

Lots were drawn for each contestant's place to perform on the program. Nero drew number four. No one seemed to pay particular attention to him during the practice session, but he watched closely in an attempt to work out who his main rivals were.

Dutifully, with Terpnus supervising, Nero proceeded to sing the required scales and play his lyre. Terpnus said nothing until it was all finished.

'You'll do well this afternoon,' he reassured Nero. 'Don't look at the audience, it's better for you if you look just above their heads and out towards the back of the theatre.'

'Then how will I know if they are enjoying listening to me?'

Terpnus gave him a smile of encouragement. 'Remember, it's not the audience but the judging panel that you should be trying to impress.' Terpnus was hoping that his pupil would not look at the audience. Otherwise, there was a good chance that he'd be overcome with fear and unable to cope.

Already, Nero was beginning to panic. Terpnus could see the rivulets of sweat running down his face.

'The session is over, we need to return to the villa,' he declared. Waiting wasn't going to be easy.

Nero was unable to eat anything and spent a perfectly miserable afternoon lying on his bed. Time seemed to stand still until he was called to ready himself for the journey back to the theatre for the performance.

The first couple of contestants weren't anything to worry about, Nero decided, as he stood watching them perform. The third, however, was. To be fair to him, he was at least of equal talent. As Nero stood listening to the judges' comments, he could feel the sweat on his hands making them slick. What if he dropped the lyre?

In the seconds before he performed, he reminded himself that he must not clear his throat as that would disqualify him.

Slowly he made his way up on to the stage. It wasn't far, but it seemed to him like a long, long way.

The first piece was based on the burning of Troy. Nero felt that he was growing in confidence and had done well. There was an outpouring of applause when he finished, especially from a special group in the theatre who'd attended for the purpose of supporting him. Unknown to the rest of the audience, they were praetorians dressed in civilian clothes. They chanted his name and stamped their feet.

It was at this time that a series of earth tremors rocked the theatre causing the judging panel to rise from their feet in alarm. Fortunately, they subsided quickly.

'Are you prepared to resume?' the head adjudicator asked Nero,' or would you prefer to postpone your performance until tomorrow?'

'I'll continue.'

A ripple of clapping went through the audience at his decision. Nero's confidence rose.

The second song went well, then suddenly it was all over and the judges retired to consider their choice of the winner. Nero stood in the theatre wings, jittery to find out how well he'd done.

Soon, the announcement came. Nero had won.

Once again, there was huge cheering from the audience. Terpnus rushed forward to be the first to congratulate his pupil. 'You must be proud, Caesar, news of this will be spoken of throughout Rome today.'

'Get me a messenger, quickly!' was his reply, 'I must let Poppy know.'

This was a moment that Nero would long remember, especially when he returned to Rome.

Later, alone in his room, Terpnus shook his head.

The second placed contestant, who had performed third, was with absolutely no doubt, far more talented than Nero.

However, if he'd been the adjudicator, Terpnus knew he would have made exactly the same decision as the judging panel.

'Tigellinus, we must return now to the villa. I'm exhausted,' Nero declared after he'd remained in the theatre accepting congratulations for a considerable length of time.

'Very well, Caesar, we'll leave immediately.'

The next morning, Nero was escorted to the best bathhouse in the city. Only the most experienced slaves assisted with his massage and personal bathing routine. The bathhouse was closed for the following three days with entry prohibited until he chose to leave the city.

Nero was delighted. Due respect had been shown to him as the talented artist that he was. And, of course, the respect due to him as Emperor. The former was by far the most important to him.

Terpnus breathed a sigh of relief.

21

Pandataria Island
Several Weeks Later

Soon, they'll come for me with their breastplates glinting in the sun and their stern gaze and my life will be over. If I'm fortunate, they might kill me with mercy but I know that is no certainty.

Octavia's prediction came true a few days later. As she looked out to sea she saw a small speck on the horizon. Her heart sank as she realised that it had to be a boat coming to Pandataria.

So, this was to be the day of her death. There was no one to witness what would happen on this day, and history would probably be silent after her life ebbed away.

Quickly, she changed into her best clothes and combed her hair. When she looked again, she could see from her window that it was indeed a boat that she'd seen. She had only to sign her name to the document and the will that she'd written and she hurried to do so. She'd stipulated that all of her remaining possessions should be given to the poor.

In the time she had left she tried to calm herself. Perhaps, this could be how she'd be remembered, as resolute and courageous, and if so, she was accepting of it. She was still young and disappointed at the loss of all the years she could have had ahead, but that was now irrelevant.

Looking down from the window she saw that the boat had reached the beach. The guards stood there in a circle surrounding their senior officer. Octavia wondered what he was saying to them, not that it mattered much now, she supposed.

'When we reach the palace remember that the lady inside is still the Empress and she is to be treated as such. I'll punish any man who shows disrespect. This is an ugly job we've been given, but we have no option and must follow our orders. There is to be not a word uttered, when we leave this island, of what happens here today. Do you understand?' The glance of Sextus, the commanding officer, swept over each man in turn, as they nodded in the affirmative.

'I'll order one of you to open the prisoner's veins so that she bleeds enough to kill her. I will then tell all but two of you to return here.'

Conscious that Octavia would have seen them arrive, he hurried to begin the ascent to the top of the cliff so as not to prolong her fear. She greeted him as he entered with his men behind him.

'I've been expecting you.'

'I regret that I must carry out my orders,' Sextus explained.

'Here is my will. There is also a document to be given to the vestals. Would you please do that for me when you return to Rome?'

'It will be my honour.'

'What is to happen now?'

'My orders are that your veins are to be opened,' I will make you as comfortable as I can.'

'Thank you. You are kind.'

'Numerius, use your gladius.'

Octavia was led to a chair and quickly her wrists were slit. She calmed after the initial sting. Sextus held her gaze and knelt down beside her. Before long, her eyes began to glaze over and he caught her as she slumped over the side of the chair and her blood began to pool around her.

'You may go, Numerius,' Sextus ordered. 'You two, stay with me.'

The manner of Octavia's death had been detailed in the orders Sextus carried, but he had absolutely no intention of carrying all of them out. It was crime enough that he should have to kill this courageous woman.

Instead of placing her in a bath of boiling hot water before she bled out, as he'd been ordered, he'd allowed her to die without going through that agony. He was unable, however, to save her from the final humiliation.

From sheer malice, after the Emperor had signed the execution order, Poppy had hidden from Nero the details she'd added of the way Octavia was to die. She'd also emphasised that she wanted Octavia's head dispatched to her in Rome.

'The two of you, our orders are to cut off the prisoner's head. I'll leave you to it. When you're finished, bring it with you after you've buried the rest of her body under the umbrella pine over there.' He pointed to a nearby tree.

Sextus was ashamed of what had occurred and his part in it, but he was a praetorian and required to carry out his orders. He was the only one to look back at this island of tears as they departed. He did so until Pandataria was only a tiny blob in the distance. He knew that however long he lived, he would never forget this day, nor would he forget Octavia's sweet face.

The next day, after his return to Rome, Sextus made his way to the Temple of Venus in the Forum. He hurried through the crowd with little resistance, due to the power his uniform afforded him.

He carried with him the will and document from Octavia. Adjacent to the temple, at the house of the vestals, he waited to see the senior vestal. As he looked out upon the pool, rose garden and statues he couldn't help thinking that Octavia would have been better off as an enclosed vestal, rather than having the life and death she'd suffered.

He pushed his thoughts aside as she approached him. Her walk was slow and dignified.

'Salve. How can I assist you?' she enquired softly.

'I have with me a will and a document from the late Empress, Octavia. I give them to you for safe-keeping as she requested.'

Before the vestal bowed her head, he thought he saw an expression of surprise and sadness cross her face. He had not realised that probably she would have been unaware yet of Octavia's death.

'I will do as she has requested,' she assured him. 'May you be blessed.' She hurried away.

The next day a package was given to Poppy at the palace. Without thinking, she opened it and found herself looking at the bloodied head of Octavia. She dropped it on the floor shrieking. 'Take this thing away from me!' Her maids arrived and horrified at what they saw, immediately informed one of the praetorians on duty who had the head removed.

Eventually, Poppy calmed down. She saw Octavia's death as a necessity for the success of her own ambitions. Having seen her severed head, at least, she told herself, she could rest assured from now on that Octavia was indeed dead.

Twelve days later Nero married Poppy. She had given him the good news that she was pregnant.

Celebrations were held throughout Rome with those holding Roman citizenship being given gifts of coins and bread. An announcement was proclaimed throughout the city:

> *Today we celebrate the marriage of our Emperor, Nero, and his new wife. We also rejoice that the Empress is expecting a child. May the gods bless and protect them!*

There was sadness on the part of some of the people. They'd been restrained from demonstrating this time, the second time that Octavia had been exiled. Severe punishments had been handed out after the first crowd riots. Now, the people had learned to be submissive and it was too late to change anything.

Poppy was absolutely thrilled that she'd reached her goals. She was married and expecting a child. She was also Rome's empress. Her only regret was that due to Aulus being indisposed, Farzana had not witnessed her triumph. Still, it was no matter, she'd make sure that she saw Farzana again very soon, then her happiness would be complete.

A lavish dinner was held at the palace. The elite of Rome attended to find themselves in a room decorated in pink. Invitations were difficult to obtain to this, one of the most important dinners of Nero's reign. Showers of rose petals fell from above as a young boy, painted the same colour, stood unmoving, providing the centrepiece of the main table which was surrounded by only the best of food and wine.

Nero had left the best until last. He stood and ordered complete silence. Everyone ceased what they were doing and looked expectantly towards the main table. When he was sure he had their complete attention, he announced:

> *I hereby bestow the title of Augusta on Poppy, your new Empress. May the gods rejoice.*

Poppy heard the applause ringing in her ears and was overcome with joy. She had successfully completed her quest to become the most wealthy and influential woman in the Roman Empire.

It was time for Poppy to bring her son, Rufrius, inside the palace. Poppy had been thinking about it for some months, but the timing hadn't been right. Poppy loved the little boy dearly, and it was unlikely that Farzana would be available on a permanent basis to look after him again. The palace wasn't exactly the perfect place for the child to live, but she needed to know he was near her.

She chose a small apartment for him, close to her own. Since Farzana had left he'd been cared for by a loving woman, Albina, whom Poppy had carefully selected at the time. The woman was close to Rufrius so she really didn't want to part them. There was room in the apartment for Albina to live in as well.

Poppy had an instinctive feeling that she should keep her son away from Nero. She couldn't have explained exactly what it was, but an innate sense of danger unsettled her. She turned, instead, to the man she thought might become a friend to her son, and give him the manly attributes he would need.

She sent for Tigellinus.

He was by necessity unmarried but honest, tough and loyal. He looked surprised when Poppy approached him.

'I know you won't have much time to give him,' she said, 'but even if it's only now and then, he needs a male around him.'

'I see.' Tigellinus did not ask the expected question. *Why not Nero?* But Poppy had already suffered the early death of a child before to Nero, so it might not be such a good idea to have Rufrius, another man's child, around him.

Tigellinus was no fool.

'I would be honoured,' he replied. Striding over to the child, who was sitting on the floor, he picked him up and swung him round and round as Rufrius squealed in delight.

Their relationship grew and became a close bond. Poppy had chosen well.

22

Tullianum Prison

'I don't know why they don't just kill you and get it over with!' the prison gaoler complained as he read the order to release Locusta. 'You're in and out of here so much it's making me giddy.' He spat on the prison floor as he ushered her out. 'And don't come back again or I'll strangle you myself!'

Locusta made a lewd gesture at him. 'You want to watch what you say around me,' she threatened, 'or you never know what poison you might find in your food!'

She enjoyed the expression of fear that spread across his face. That should spoil his enjoyment of what he ate for a while, she inwardly congratulated herself.

She laughed as she ambled out the door. No doubt, it was Nero who'd released her as she'd hoped he would. There was probably someone he was thinking of poisoning soon.

At least, while she was in prison, she'd had plenty of time to think. Much as Locusta liked the idea of buying the house on the Aventine, she'd decided that she'd leave the city and go out to the fringes of Rome. There she'd buy a place to live in and also set up the school she'd wanted to open for so long. The money she had would also purchase more on the edge of Rome than it would in the centre of the city.

Hitching up her long tunic out of the dirt, she continued to walk until she'd left the city behind and found herself on a road on her own. Once she got used to the quietness, she began to enjoy it, and vowed that she'd never live in the city again. Now, all she had to do was to find a suitable building to buy. She realised that she'd started to limp due to all of the walking.

Locusta was lucky that after a few enquiries to people who lived in the area, she was able to find the perfect place. She bought it with the gold coins she'd saved over so many years, and still had sufficient savings left over to make the changes she wanted.

After several months of hard work, she began to circulate word around Rome that she'd train others in her skill if they paid for it. There was no shortage of applicants and as time passed the numbers were such, that she found herself turning people away.

Those who came to her were surprised to find a tidy and presentable, even comfortable central building, with large, tended gardens where herbs and spices and also many other plants grew. The very few who had seen Locusta in the past were astounded in the change in her. Gone was the long, unwashed hair and the dirty, old robe she had worn. Now her hair was clean, tied back and tidy and she wore a spotless, white tunic.

They'd expected to find a run-down old building in poor condition but most of all without any of the necessary services. Instead they found clean washing and drinking water and comfortable seating.

Locusta taught her students well, showing them how to prepare potions for their deadly purpose. She was still an angel of death.

'The practical part of your study here is, of course, the most important,' she told them one day in the first of the practical lectures. 'It will take you some years of experience to know exactly what poison suits any particular victim, especially due to the relevant circumstances. There will nearly always be the problem of discovery. Make a mistake and it may cost you your life!'

Locusta looked around the ring of students in front of her and their serious faces pleased her. She was gaining real satisfaction from passing on her knowledge.

'You see around you all of the plants that you'll be working with. I will be giving you information on what dosage to give for use on victims of your potions.'

The students nodded their understanding.

'Can any of you give me the name of a type of potion that you might use to poison someone?' Several students raised their hands.

'Belladonna.'

'And another?'

'Cyanide'

'Very good. Obviously, there are also others. Beware the plant that is beautiful. There are two you need to particularly consider. The first is the Oleander. Its flowers are a pretty pink and it's so innocent to look at, but wash your hands well after touching any part of it. The other is Aconite which has vivid blue, almost purple flowers. Its poison can be deadly.'

Locusta's students were very keen to do well. She had no problems with the practical side of her instruction, as victims were said to have been supplied to her. These were people who were criminals and the scum off the streets.

'How many people have you killed?' one of Locusta's more adventurous students asked her one day.

'Take care when asking such questions,' she replied glaring at him, 'I'll teach all of you some of my methods but you'll never know all of them.'

The student sank back quickly in his seat.

It did set Locusta thinking, however. How many had she poisoned? Was it dozens or hundreds? She ticked off some of them on her fingers, especially the important ones like Britannicus. Placing the poison in his water was a master stroke. She smiled and lifted her chin.

Hers was an art.

What she did know, was that by the time all of her students had passed through her school, there would probably be thousands more dead. Perhaps, she'd even become more famous than she was already.

Part III

The Secret

23

ROME

The Palatine
19 July 64 A.D.

At first it was just a teasing, yellowish red flicker-a small insignificant 'something,' lick, lick, licking at the edges of a rotten, sagging piece of the furniture factory's ancient timber door. It was a tiny pulse of light in the dark night that had already fallen, concealing the squalor of the buildings near the Circus Maximus and their occupants' shady transactions, as well as their more vile, human transgressions.

The narrow laneway lay empty, foul and silent except for one old vagrant at its far end, coughing and shuffling on shaky legs as he disappeared from sight around the corner. The transformation when it came was swift and startling. From the rags of decrepit old age emerged a youthful figure, moving fast.

A pile of discarded rags lay strewn on the paving stones.

Further up the laneway behind him the tiny, pulsing flicker was also undergoing a transformation. From an existence barely more than nothingness, it eventually became the raging flames of a relentless, killer inferno, hungry to devour the great city of Rome.

Antium
South of Rome

Poppy lay half asleep, enjoying the cooling breeze through the window, as it whispered against her skin. Her eyes fluttered open as Nero entered the bedroom.

'Are you feeling better?' he asked anxiously.

'A little,' she smiled. 'It's just the pregnancy. I love this place, I'd like to come here more often.'

He bent to kiss her. 'Whatever makes you happy.'

'Thank you. I think I'll take a short walk later to the temple. The fresh air will do me good.'

The small gem of a temple, the Temple of Neptune, stood in total silence and unoccupied when Poppy reached it. She sat silently appreciating the interior with its beautiful and fragile frescoes, mosaics and statues.

Her mind went back in time to the beginning of her journey. For Poppy, that was the day she'd married Rufrius. So very much had happened since then. With a feeling of wonder, she realised that the passionate drive for revenge that had fuelled all of her efforts had lessened a little.

The peace that she'd sought for so long lay within her reach. She'd travel to her villa at Oplontis to see Farzana and enjoy being there again. Also, she very much wanted to return to Pompeii. Perhaps, this should be in the near future.

That night, as she sat with Nero, a messenger reached them after an urgent ride from Rome. He handed Nero a message from Tigellinus:

Caesar,

Rome is burning. May I suggest that you return with haste.

Tigellinus

'How bad is it?' Nero asked the messenger.

'Caesar, it's being said that this fire is the worst to ever ravage the city.'

It was agreed that Nero would ride immediately for Rome. Poppy would travel the next day by carriage. She endured a sleepless night, wondering how bad the fire was. She had no desire to see the city in ruins.

A huge, red sun greeted the new day in Rome with disdain, the smell of smoke thick in the air and oppressive heat. The flames took the path of least resistance moving along the open ground that lay towards the Palatine Hill. It passed over the underground Temple of Mithras and through the areas with no brick boundaries to contain it, until it was headed towards the Forum.

The fire respected neither the gods nor patricians and certainly not the common people. It swept through temples, villas and gardens, badly damaging the royal palace which lay in its path.

Narrow laneways with high wooden insulae built close to the street aided the fire's progress as it attacked the apartments of the common people. Terrified, they tumbled and ran from the buildings screaming, and as the huge crowd attempted to flee, people impeded each other, pushing, shoving, falling, until some were injured and others, old or disabled, were left behind. There were some, however, at that time who did aid those unable to help themselves.

The noise and chaos were frightening.

Many fled the centre of the city and ran through the city gates sheltering in tombs and even open countryside on the fringes of Rome. The cohortes vigilum, responsible for responding to fires in Rome, worked valiantly with their pumps and axes to put out the blaze, but were hindered by an unknown group intent on stopping them.

For six days the fire devastated the city, being brought to an end by a windbreak, constructed on the Esquiline Hill. The people who owned the houses to be used as fill, helped to tear their own homes down.

Earlier, the fire appeared to have been stopped, but it restarted in the garden of the estate of Tigellinus. It was known afterwards that a group of men threw burning torches into the fire when it seemed that it was going out. No one knew who they were, except that they'd shouted that they, 'had their orders.'

Of the fourteen precincts of Rome, only four were untouched by fire. These were the Jewish sections of the city. It was noted that within two years after the fire, the people of Judea rioted against Rome's rule.

Nero dismounted from his horse as they reached a high point overlooking Rome. The sight he saw horrified him. Flames were everywhere it seemed. Yellow and red dancing demons, they raced forward seeking destruction. As he rode beside Tigellinus into the city Nero saw people running, not knowing where they were going as long as it was away from the fire.

'Tigellinus, we must see what can be done. Have the remainder of your guards help to stop the path of the fire and also guide people through to safety. All of us must do our best!' Dismounting, he moved into the midst of the chaos helping some of those fleeing or lying injured in the streets. By the time they'd finished, he was bruised and covered in soot and ashes.

Tigellinus looked at him with a new respect.

Rome was a sorry sight when the fire was eventually out and new problems had to be solved. Poppy returned to Rome to live in the damaged palace.

'Who can have done this?' she asked Nero, shaking her head. 'There are even rumours in the streets, I've heard them myself, that you actually gave orders to light the fire. It's not true, surely!'

'Of course, it's not true,' he reassured her, but you know we must find out who did light it if these rumours are to be stopped!'

Tigellinus, who was also in the room, had remained silent until then. 'I believe that you are correct,' he agreed. 'We must find out who could have done it.'

'My opinion is that it was the Jews,' Nero declared. 'The fire didn't touch their section of the city, and they also have some strange prophecy about Rome burning.'

'It's far more likely to have been the Christians,' Poppy retorted accusingly.

'With respect, the Christians aren't even worth considering,' Tigellinus countered. 'There are very few of them. They're a small group of people with weird ideas but they don't have a history of violence. I predict, however, that Rome will have further trouble with the Jews in future.'

'I'm sorry, Tigellinus but I disagree with you,' Poppy insisted.

'I'm going to have to think about this,' Nero hesitated.

'That's all well and good,' Tigellinus told him, 'but don't take too long!'

He stood alone when the Prefect had gone, silently surveying what remained of the city around him. He no longer saw the ravages of the fire but a vision of a new Rome. He'd widen the streets, move the insulae back away from the footpaths, and have the new buildings built of brick. And as for the centre of the city, he'd make it the most beautiful city in the world.

Nero felt elated. This was an opportunity he could not resist. The people would have their new city and he would have a palace of gold with lakes, fountains and gardens. And the people would praise him. Rome would be the most stunning city in the Empire.

'This is no place for you, my dear. I strongly suggest that you travel to Campania where you'll be safe,' Nero told Poppy the next morning.

'Perhaps you're right,' she sighed. 'Are you sure there's nothing I can help with here?'

'It's better that you don't have to worry about it.'

Poppy nodded that she agreed with him. Soon after, she departed the city, away from the dead, the broken dreams and the devastation and she was glad to go.

During the days that followed, the Guard as well as the palace administrators worked long hours trying to provide stability and begin to re-build the city. Virtually all of Rome including the Forum district was nothing but a huge, smoking catastrophe.

Long tables were set up with basic food for the many citizens who had nothing. Other items such as clothing had to be found as many in Rome had lost absolutely everything. The Tiber became a place for survivors to wash off the grime, soot and blood that had resulted from the fire and the injuries many had suffered.

'We must open my private gardens for the people to use,' Nero ordered Tigellinus, as they walked through the devastation attempting to find anything that appeared it could be salvaged to begin the re-building.

The order was passed to a nearby praetorian. 'Fixing all of this is going to take a very long time,' Tigellinus warned.

'Well, we have to start somewhere,' Nero continued, 'but I have to agree, there's not much left to begin with.'

He turned his attention to the treasury finances, harassing his administrators to find new sources of wealth to use in the rebuilding. Surely, there had to be a way to raise the funds. Then, a thought came to him. There was one way to raise great wealth and he decided to use it.

As vast land clearing continued and work began on Nero's new, extravagant palace of gold, he began a purge of the wealthy, not only in Rome but also in Africa. Proscription lists were drawn up of prominent, wealthy men who were promptly executed and their wealth confiscated. The funds for the building of Nero's dreams began to roll in.

The Royal Palace

The hammering went on throughout the late afternoon. legionaries pounded large, wooden posts into the earth outside the palace windows overlooking the lush, green lawn. The ground was moist and yielding from recent heavy rain which made the task somewhat easier. Inside, slaves scurried about their duties in preparation for the evening ahead.

As dusk fell, the legionaries returned with coils of rope. Soon after, they led out six Christian captives and proceeded to tie them firmly to the wooden posts. They were each then liberally daubed with tar. Inside the palace, oil lamps were left unlit so that the interior was almost in darkness.

Night fell.

At Nero's signal, slaves carrying flaming torches began to light the human captives. This was carried out slowly, one by one, so as to prolong the terror of each victim for the entertainment of those watching. Soon, flames lit up the night as their agonised screams rang out in the silence.

When it was over, Nero ordered the palace lamps to be lit, music to be played and dinner laid out for the invited guests who had witnessed the whole ordeal through the palace windows. He also proceeded to engage various visitors in pleasant conversation, apparently completely oblivious to the impact on them of the scene that had just been enacted in front of them.

The message was clear to those senators hostile to the Emperor. They, too, could expect to meet a similar fate if they dared to conspire against him, and news would also filter through to the common people of what awaited them if they dared to oppose Nero.

Standing behind the closed double doors that prevented entry to the reception room, Poppy stood watching and listening. Two senators not realising that they were standing only feet away from her on the other side of the door spoke their minds.

'Nero's a monster,' the younger senator stated in a shocked voice.

'Yes, but don't be misled,' the other replied, his voice lowered. 'I have absolutely no doubt whatever that this spectacle tonight was due to the influence of the Empress.'

'Why?'

'Just think about it. She's a devout Jewess. There's no doubt that the Jews started the fire and she'll defend them.'

Poppy slipped quietly away, ready to depart the city. She'd spend several days at the villa in Baiae then return. The torching of the victims was not something she'd enjoyed, but she knew from experience that she had to look after those who were loyal to her, because that was all she had, and this had been the only way to do it.

Alone in Baiae, Poppy tried to rationalise her decision. Someone had to die to deflect any criticism away from Nero and from the Jews for the fire. Had what she'd done been so wrong to deflect blame from one group to another?

She made her way down to the beach and took solitary walks along the strip of sand, enjoying the feeling between her toes. Niggling at her remained the knowledge that she was desperately seeking to deny. Each of the people who'd died such a horrible death was innocent and there was no way of explaining that away.

24

Nero stared intently at the model on the desk in front of him as his architects, Severus and Celer, stood nearby watching anxiously. Since the Great Fire, their every waking moment had been spent attempting to meet the Emperor's demands for the building of the new Domus Aurea. With his present palace the Domus Transitoria on the Palatine badly damaged, and parts of it burnt beyond recognition, Nero had announced that he'd decided to construct not only a new palace, but one that was beyond anyone's imagination.

As if that wasn't enough, most of central Rome was to be transformed into parks and gardens as well as a huge lake

for the use of the Emperor and also the public. Exotic animals would be brought in from the rest of the Empire for the people to marvel at.

There was a great deal of chatter and speculation amongst the common people of Rome. Some saw an opportunity for an improvement to their lives. Most, however, whinged and

Daughter of Pompeii

whined that the Emperor had robbed them of their public spaces to use for his own private estate.

Still others wondered if Nero had started the fire. Perhaps it had been Tigellinus whose men had been seen throwing flaming torches into the already burning buildings. If that was the case, had the Emperor known?

The whole Domus Aurea construction was presently in the early stages of completion, but already the enormity of Nero's dream was apparent. Severus and Celer could only wring their hands with anxiety and frustration and hope that whatever plans they put before the Emperor would please him.

'It's simply too small!' Nero frowned. 'The lake isn't big enough and you've not allowed sufficient space around the colossal statue at the entry to be properly appreciated. I want visitors to be enthralled from the moment they arrive!'

'Of course, Caesar,' Celer answered, 'we'll change the plans to reflect your wishes.'

'Also,' Nero added as the architects stood wondering what additional impossible requirements he'd come up with, 'Poppy wishes the bedroom door in her apartment to be able to open out at the back. This will allow her to sit in the portico and watch the fountain and the lagoon.'

'What fountain? What lagoon?' Celer whispered behind his hand.

'I don't know.' Severus felt sick in the stomach. Poppy had been scathing when she'd last spoken to them. Her manner could be arrogant and abrasive at the best of times, and their most recent discussion with her had been an unmitigated disaster.

'As you wish, Caesar,' Celer managed to mutter.

'You may go.'

They hurried away as Nero returned to his contemplation of the plans. Why couldn't they see his vision? Why did he have to explain every little detail so that he got what he wanted? His Golden Palace would eclipse anything ever built and his vision would be marvelled at down the years to come. But it was all so exhausting!

He turned to gaze out of the window. The rebuilding of the city following the devastation from the fire was progressing slowly. The wider streets and additional fire protections would increase safety in the city, but there was still so much to be done. He sighed with frustration.

Tigellinus, Prefect of the Guard, had been lounging unobserved by the doorway for several minutes. Now, he moved into the room as he guessed at the Emperor's mood. For self-protection, he'd decided when first elevated to his present position, that it paid to be one step ahead of Nero at all times.

'I see you are making new changes to the plans for the golden palace,' Tigellinus commented in a voice that was carefully non-judgemental. 'It must be tiring for you to carry the weight of such a large project on your shoulders.'

'You're one of the few that understands the demands on me,' Nero replied gratefully. 'I feel drained by the constant need to oversight everything. Does no one else have any creative talent?'

'Yes, but they don't have your natural instincts. You will have to persevere alone, if necessary, if you ever wish to see this project completed.'

Tigellinus was tough, intelligent and loyal. He was also one of very few that Nero truly trusted. His toughness was backed up by a large physique and great skill with a gladius.

'Come. Let's walk.' Nero led the way across the parklands where labourers were hard at work creating a garden paradise. 'What did you want to discuss with me?' he asked as they reached the edge of the excavation for the lake.

'We do have one problem, Caesar,' Tigellinus began, 'and unfortunately, it's a large one.'

'Explain.'

Daughter of Pompeii

'The treasury coffers are beginning to empty at an alarming rate. The way things are going, we'll run out of funds before the project is finished.'

Nero was thoughtful as Tigellinus waited for his reaction.

'Does that include the funds from the African proscriptions and new taxes levied in Moesia?' he asked.

'I'm afraid it does,' Tigellinus answered. 'We must find funds from another source.'

Nero thought for a minute or two then he smiled unexpectedly.

'Gold is coming from Alexandria. I expect it to arrive very soon at Portus. It's enough to keep us going, at least for a while. I'd almost forgotten about it.'

He walked over to speak to a couple of the workmen. Not for the first time Tigellinus wondered at his popularity with many of the common people, especially when he was hated so much by Rome's senators and patricians. He watched as awe spread across the workers' faces. He had no doubt that Nero had just provided them with a story that their families would feast on for decades to come.

Poppy was definitely irritated.

She'd succeeded in subtly influencing Nero to exile his popular wife, Octavia, to the island of Pandataria before eventually executing her. But Poppy wasn't sure now that she'd become Rome's empress, that the outcome was quite what she'd expected. Perhaps it was Nero's persistent obsession with his Golden Palace. Maybe, it was the dreary weather. Or, perhaps it was the constant stress of playing the role of a loving wife as well as nausea from her current pregnancy. Either way, Poppy was ready for a change, and it didn't include her husband.

The answer came to her suddenly and she wondered why she hadn't done something about it sooner. She'd talk Nero into a journey alone somewhere, anywhere, the further away the better. She'd take time to travel away from Rome herself, away from him and his problems. That would no doubt help to dispel her boredom. She'd even consider making it an official visit for part of the time, so that the people could see her.

With the help of her maid, Layla, she immediately set about the task of sorting through her wardrobe and selecting those clothes that would be suitable for travelling to Pompeii and attending functions there. She'd have a lovely, long stay at her villa at Oplontis for the first time.

It sounded like utter bliss!

Poppy broached the subject that night over dinner.

'How are the plans progressing, my love?' she asked.

'Not well, I'm sorry to say. The architects are slow to understand what I want and we've barely got some of the foundations started so far.'

'Time away to freshen up and relax might help you,' she suggested.

'That's not such a bad idea, but where?'

'Somewhere you've neglected to visit, but definitely should. I believe you can confidently leave work for the architects and workmen to be done in your absence.'

Intrigued, Nero turned to offer her figs that had been placed on the table for dessert. 'I can't imagine where that would be. Now, you've got me wondering.'

Poppy gave him a warm smile. 'It's a place to prepare you for travel to a country that deserves to be made aware of your talent,' she teased.

'Where?'

'Portus. As you know it has a very large amphitheatre on the outskirts as well as flat, open fields perfect for days of practice, and there is comfortable accommodation nearby in Ostia. Your second journey, when you are better prepared, would be to Greece.' It took only a few moments for Poppy to see that her choice had been a good one.

'You know me so well, Poppy,' Nero reached out to brush her arm lightly with his hand. 'Of course, you're right. I'd enjoy that and it would freshen me up for when I return. I'd need to take quite a large retinue, though. It will have to include the trainers, grooms and others. You don't think that's too many do you?'

'Certainly not. I wouldn't think that's a problem,' Poppy replied. 'If anything, it will be good for Romans outside the city to watch you race, and it won't do any harm for you to take a number of supporters with you.'

'Tigellinus!'

'Yes, Caesar.'

'How do you think some of your guards would feel about giving me protection as I practice in the amphitheatre at Portus? It would be every day for some time.'

'I didn't know you were contemplating that,' the praetorian commander replied.

'Well, I am now.' Nero cast a grateful look at Poppy as he waited for an answer.

'There are certainly enough of them who would be willing and grateful to do it I would think, Caesar.'

Tigellinus neglected to include himself but Nero was so excited that he didn't notice.

'I've just had a thought,' Poppy continued, with the full attention of her husband. 'You do have one senior administrator with the experience to make decisions here until your return. What about Helius?'

'He's perfect, my dear. He would have a steady hand on affairs here in Rome and he wouldn't aspire to actions above his level of responsibility. This will be an important preparation period. The orders must be given urgently to those who'll need to attend meetings to make the necessary arrangements.'

'That's a very good idea,' Poppy agreed.

'Send for the messenger! I need to advise the officials at Portus,' Nero ordered, 'as soon as possible.'

The Greens Training Stable
(Outside Rome)

'Have my horses ready for me, Aelianus, I must begin to practise tomorrow.' Nero stood talking with one of the trainers responsible for the horses in the Green faction of professional charioteers who performed at the Circus Maximus.

'Certainly, Caesar.'

'I'll be competing in our next major festival here and I must train now to be ready in time. At the moment we can start with just the team of four, but before I go, I must learn to handle a bigger team.'

'How many horses did you have in mind?'

'I'm not sure yet, but certainly at least four, probably six, and maybe even more.'

The trainer was obviously surprised.

'I must improve my skills to impress Rome's citizens,' Nero continued. 'It's important that I put on a good display.'

'You'll be coming here more often to practice then, Caesar?'

'Beginning tomorrow I'll be here most mornings, unless something else really urgent requires my attention. Before I go, I'd like to see my horses.'

'Yes, Caesar. Please follow me.'

They walked towards the large stables where the horses were held. A couple of teams were already out on the practice track and Nero stopped for a couple of minutes to watch them before going in to see his own horses. These were inferior to his, he knew. The problem was to find others so that he could drive a bigger team. They were a magnificent team of matching white horses, presently being groomed. Nero smiled as he strode towards them.

'Well, my children, have you been working hard,' he asked softly. One of them came up to him snuffling into his hand.

'Look after them well!' he ordered the trainer before turning to leave.

'Caesar, it may be that we need more security, we've been finding curse tablets in the stables,' the trainer told him, 'I have one here.' He handed it to Nero who held it in his hand and read it:

> *I adjure you, demon, whoever you are, and I demand of you from this hour, from this day, from this moment that you torture and kill the horses of the Greens and Whites*

Nero frowned. 'Have there been any other incidents lately?'

'Not that I know about.'

'We don't need the kind of man who'd write this, coming anywhere near the horses. I'll have two guards sent here each night to make sure no one causes trouble.'

There was an expression of relief on the face of the trainer. It wouldn't do to have anything happen to any of the Emperor's "children."

That evening Nero and Poppy discussed his journey to Portus. He'd be absent from Rome for a considerable period of time. That posed certain dangers.

'I hope that no one feels they can take advantage of my absence,' he frowned.

Poppy reassured him, 'if they do, they can always be dealt with by Tigellinus,' she suggested. 'And Portus isn't that far from here. The difficult one will be the second trip, to Greece.'

Nero's frown lifted. 'Yes. That is possible in conjunction with Helius.'

'I will also be absent,' Poppy reminded him. 'I've left it far too long without paying an *official* visit to Pompeii.'

She emphasised the word "official." 'This will give me an opportunity to do that.'

The arrangements were made with an understanding that if there was real trouble in Rome, Nero would return. If that happened, however, it would take several days of travel. The decision for Nero to leave had been taken, however, and would not be changed.

25

POMPEII

Farzana sat amongst the bluebells that grew wild in profusion on the banks of the river Sarno. She'd hitched up her tunic just a little and her long legs dangled over the riverbank into the cool, shallow stream.

Aeneus sat beside her unpacking the food he'd bought from one of the street vendor stalls. Then, he sensed her eyes on him.

'I've never spoken to you about Poppy, Aeneus, have I?' Farzana asked.

He glanced across at her. 'I don't think so.'

'I believe, perhaps, that it's time I did.' She paused and he waited for her to begin.

'Poppy is my best friend, she's more like a sister. We met here some years ago as we were both born in Pompeii. This is not an ordinary friendship and she's a large part of my life.'

'Go on.'

'The first thing you need to know is that she is Empress of Rome.'

Farzana saw Aeneus' eyes widen in shock and he nearly choked on his food as he spluttered and took in the information.

'Are you joking?' he asked with a light laugh.

'No. This is how it all started...'

Farzana told their story as she knew it until the present day. The remainder of their lunch lay forgotten on the riverbank as Aeneus sat unmoving, enthralled by what he was hearing.

Eventually, Farzana stopped speaking and for a moment neither of them said anything, until Aeneus broke the silence. He paused for a moment as if searching for words.

'I'm so pleased for you.' You're both very lucky to have found each other. Do you think the Empress of Rome would object if I asked you to marry me?'

Farzana burst into tears.

'I hope they're happy tears?'

'They are. My answer is *yes* and I'm sure Poppy will be overjoyed for us.'

It took a little time for the somewhat over-awed expression to leave Aeneus' face. He kissed her tenderly and they knew that their love would last.

'Poppy's sure to be coming here soon, probably for a quiet visit, so only my family and now you, will know who she is. Don't worry, she's very easy to talk to and when she's here she's still the girl I knew all those years ago, except that life since then has changed her just a little. You will keep everything you see and hear secret, won't you?'

'You can trust me. As I'm leaving the praetorians soon, at least she won't be able to demote me,' Aeneus joked.

'That's a story for another day.' Farzana laughed at the bewildered look on his face. 'I'll explain later. There's plenty of time,' she told him.

'A messenger came while you were gone,' Aulus informed Farzana when she returned. He handed her the scroll.

'It's from Poppy. She says that she wants to be out of Rome for a while. She's also missing Pompeii. She'll be coming here very soon for an official visit so that people can come to talk to her. She'll be staying at the Inn of Sulpicii so as not to disturb us. That's the best hotel and it screens its guests. I'm sure when they hear that Poppy is coming it won't be a problem for them to provide her with a beautiful suite and a private triclinium and bath. Security and privacy is very good there, too.

When the official visit is finished she'll go to live at her villa at Oplontis. She's asked that I have it ready for her arrival, and wants to know if I can make time to stay there with her for a while so she has company. I hope that she might ask you to visit one day, Aeneus. You won't believe what the villa is like unless you see it all.'

Farzana, Aeneus and Aulus looked at one another, surprise still on their faces. Farzana handed the message to Aulus to read.

'That's unexpected,' Farzana commented, 'especially the official visit. I knew that Poppy would come back here soon, but not the rest of it. I wonder if something is wrong in Rome?'

'Who knows. You can guess what things are like there,' Aeneus commented. 'I'm sure she'll tell you all about it when she gets here.'

'You don't mind do you, Aeneus, if I spend time with Poppy before she returns to Rome?'

Aeneus shook his head. 'I'm sure I can manage that, but just for you,' he joked.

'Congratulations!' Aulus shook Aeneus by the hand. 'I appreciated that you asked for my permission before proposing to my daughter.'

'So, you knew all the time, father!' Farzana pretended annoyance before beginning to laugh. 'How do you know I accepted?'

'I just know,' he said, pleased with himself. 'And you did, didn't you!'

The following days were happy for them with memories that lasted a lifetime. Together, Farzana and Aeneus began immediately to arrange for the necessary staff to be available to look after Poppy at her villa.

'What about security?' Aeneus asked. 'Do you think I should arrange something myself through my barracks?'

'It might be a good idea to warn them, though I'm not sure if that will be enough.'

'I'm working tomorrow so I'll see to it then.'

'I'm going up to look inside and open the villa for a couple of hours and make sure everything she likes has been arranged for when she arrives,' Farzana explained. 'If you'd like to come with me you could wait in the garden while I go in. As well as I know Poppy, I still wouldn't take anyone else inside without asking her.'

That afternoon they took a carriage the short distance to Oplontis and entered through the villa's gates. Aeneus had the expected response as they drove up the drive.

'This is incredible,' he exclaimed, 'what a magnificent place and I can hear the sea.'

'I told you,' Farzana looked pleased with herself, 'but I knew you had to see it for yourself. And you haven't even been inside yet. Why don't you look around the garden and pool and if you like you can take the cliff path that overlooks the sea.'

A little later, that was where Farzana found him when she'd finished and locked the villa door. They stood together looking over the ocean and Aeneus put his arm around her waist.

'This is a special place,' Aeneus whispered 'and so is our love. Surely, it will last for ever.'

The next morning Farzana returned to the villa to oversight the workmen. She found the gardener busy in the internal garden, the painters at work on the walls inside and others outside deciding how to fill the enormous pool. More gardeners were maintaining paths and the outside gardens.

'Salve, Hinnulus, you're here early.'

'Salve, Farzana. I know you've already had me paint some frescoes here recently, but there's still a great deal more to be done. As you can see, my son is already painting some of the walls that needed work. What do you think?'

Farzana studied the new frescoes and the Pompeii red being applied to one of the walls. Her gaze went to the peacock painted at an earlier time.

'I really like it,' Farzana told him. 'Hinnulus, would you be sure to retouch the peacock and the theatre mask. They look a little worn to me.'

She walked on and nodded her approval as she stopped to watch his son. 'I love the red, and it's offset so beautifully by the golden colour beside it. It's lovely workmanship!' She smiled at him and he flushed with embarrassment.

A workman was down on his hands and knees replacing broken tesserae on the Hercules mosaic in the caldarium. 'Salve, Lady. I believe this is beginning to look more the way it should,' he grinned up at her.

'It certainly is,' Farzana praised him. 'When will you finish?'

'Sometime today.'

The kitchen had been thoroughly cleaned as she'd requested and a new mortarium and pestle stood on the well-scrubbed table together with an extensive selection of Samian crockery. Beautifully decorated silverware to drink from stood beside it.

Farzana wandered outside to where a bird bath standing near a stone bench was being cleaned, watched over by a giant plane tree. Several more of them and some lemon trees stood in the back garden. Walking further, she came to two enclosed courtyards.

'How very pretty,' she murmured as she noted the frescoes that had been painted on the walls. One had its own narrow, rectangular pool lined with statues. Only now did she realise how little of the estate she'd originally seen.

Returning inside, Farzana decided to check if the beds and linens had been delivered. She wondered which of the two largest cubicula Poppy would have chosen for herself, taking a guess that it would probably have been the one with the wonderful view of the sea. In comparison, the other had a restful view of an expanse of garden.

She chose the room with the view of the sea.

The final touch to be added once everything had been completed would be numerous vases of freshly cut Pompeii roses. They would come from her own garden. Farzana had done her best.

26

The Basilica
The forum

Clodius Flaccus, Duumvir of Pompeii, wrung his hands with anxiety. A short, rotund man, nearly bald, he was dressed in a tunic with a gold cord around his middle and wore a chunky, gold symbol of office hung around his neck. He'd already served two terms as Duumvir and at this present moment was decidedly leaning towards this being his last. He stared out at the broken pavement of the city's large forum.

The sight was not a pretty one.

An earthquake several years before, the worst in living memory in the city, had ruined the beauty of the forum and just about everything in it, including statues of gods and important citizens, columns and parts of the temples of Jupiter and Apollo.

Shattered fragments of the statues that had lined the perimeter still lay smashed and broken. It was a sad sight.

The council had decided to use marble this time to re-pave the whole area. The problem was that only part of it had been done, and there was no way all of the remainder could be finished before the official visit.

'Can we at least have the workmen put marble down in an area near the entrance to the forum where we can greet the Empress when she arrives?'

'I'll get a group of the men to begin this morning,' the works supervisor offered. 'I'm fairly confident we can at least finish that much. At least all of the fountains are working again except, of course, for some of those in private residences.'

The whole city had responded to the news of Poppy's visit. Their pride was shared by all, that one of their own had actually reached her elevated status. They co-operated with each other in making sure that Pompeii looked at its best, at least, the best it could look, given the repairs still needing to be done following the earthquake. Even the broken sun dial in the forum had been replaced.

A group of gardeners stood nearby waiting to have duties allocated for the day. They'd brought their rakes, hoes and axes with them as well as a couple of handcarts to carry away rubbish.

'I want you to work in the gardens at the Temple of Venus today. The Empress is certain to wish to visit there. Pay particular attention to the flower gardens and remove any rubbish. You can start now. Time left over in the afternoon can be used to begin cleaning up the footpaths and streets, and don't forget to clean and shine the street shrines, both inside and out. We don't wish to show any disrespect to the gods.'

Clodius hurried inside the spacious Basilica to meet with Vibius, one of the city's scribes and the council members. They waited for him to be seated.

Daughter of Pompeii

'Has the list been finished yet of those being invited to attend the official welcome dinner and lunch and also the speakers?' the Duumvir asked hopefully.

'We've just finished,' one of the councillors answered as he handed the scroll to Clodius. 'What we haven't decided yet, though, is the main speaker for the evening. It's not an easy decision,' he frowned.

'I really can't see the problem,' Clodius grunted, a surprised expression on his face. 'I would have thought that the answer was obvious. We should choose Senator Diomedes.'

'You wouldn't rather have Caecilius Jucundus do it?' suggested one of the other councillors. 'He was rather interested in volunteering for it when it was mentioned.'

'He holds too much of the power in this city already,' Clodius snapped. 'No! I won't have it! This should be offered to a distinguished citizen, not necessarily the richest! Not that Senator Diomedes isn't wealthy, but Jucundus is far more so. Jucundus may attend the lunch. He should direct his efforts to his banking business and all the other honorary positions he holds in this town. How much wealth and status does one person need!'

Clodius had become quite red in the face during this outburst. There was silence around the table. He made an effort and re-gathered and calmed himself. 'So, we're all in agreement, are we?' he looked sharply around the group. No one objected and the completed list was handed to Vibius.

'Be sure to use only the best materials when you write this list, Vibius. It's important that those invited feel they have been granted an honour.'

Vibius took it and left.

The Gentlemen's Club
House of the Centenary

Clodius had two more important tasks. Slipping out of the Basilica's side door he stepped into Via Stabiana and began walking towards the Venus district, but stopped before arriving there and made his way instead to The Gentlemen's Club.

'Salve, Clodius,' the owner, Sempronius called to him as he entered. The Duumvir was, of course, a club member. He sighed and slumped down into one of the comfortable chairs.

'Having a hard day?' Sempronius asked sympathetically.

'It's going to be nearly impossible to get everything ready before Poppy gets here,' he muttered. Picking up one of the plumped-up cushions he placed it behind his aching back.

'Well, I suppose that you can only do your best. She's one of our own, so she won't be looking for faults.'

'That's true,' Clodius smiled slightly. 'I'd quite forgotten that in the middle of all the madness. I think she's probably just looking forward to being home again.'

'Can I get you a drink?'

'I'd like a cool beaker of wine, please. And don't water it down!'

'I wouldn't dream of it,' Sempronius grinned.

'Also, is Prima here?'

'She's busy at the moment but I think she's due to finish very soon. Actually, here she comes now.' Sempronius left with a nod at Prima.

'Salve, Clodius. It's good to see you again,' Prima greeted him. 'Are you here to see me?'

'I am, Prima. You know most of the people around here, don't you?'

'Yes,' Prima frowned. 'Is there trouble?'

'No, not yet. You know the Empress will be here for a visit in a couple of days?'

'Yes.'

'Do me a favour will you, and spread the word, if you or any of the street girls see anything out of place, like a robbery or something, let someone at the basilica know and we'll attend to it. I'd prefer to keep everything quiet and pleasant as much as I can.'

'Willingly,' Prima smiled. 'That's the least I can do.'

Villa of Diomedes
Outside the Herculaneum Gate

Clodius had one more visit to make before thinking about lunch. Leaving Prima, he made his way towards Via Consolare and the Herculanium Gate. The streets were busy but gradually grew quieter the further he walked. Opening the gate at the top of several steps leading into the property of Lucius Diomedes, Clodius paused to admire the appearance of the house and front garden.

Lucius, the young senator representing Pompeii, appeared at the door himself and stepped forward eagerly to grasp Clodius' hand. 'I believe we have an official visit to look forward to,' he greeted the Duumvir. 'How are preparations coming along?'

'You wouldn't like to undertake to carry them out instead of me, would you?' Clodius grimaced.

'I'm sorry, I can't help you there,' Lucius shook his head. 'Come inside and we can talk. I believe you mentioned something about a dinner speech.'

The two men spent the next hour sitting in comfort drinking wine in the peristyle garden at the back of Lucius' villa. The garden had been restored to its original beauty so that no reminder remained of the earthquake. It was a large area well maintained and attractive with olive and mulberry trees. They discussed the dinner and agreed on the time and place.

Clodius feared that if he stayed there gazing out at the fountain much longer, he would drift off to sleep and lose any possibility of finishing his urgent afternoon tasks.

'Just one more thing,' Lucius asked as he accompanied Clodius to the front gate, 'what have you done about city security?'

'Nothing yet.'

'Leave that to me,' Lucius offered. An advance notification may not be enough. They can be slack with matters like this. I'll officially arrange for more praetorians from Nuceria on the city streets to make sure that there are no problems.'

Clodius was grateful. He knew that he couldn't possibly finish everything, but at least now, he had one less problem to worry about.

An Inn
Vicolo di Frontone

Varus opened one bleary eye then quickly closed it again with a groan, as he became aware once more of the run-down room in which he lived. Then he remembered. He swung his legs over the side of the bed. The Empress was coming in a couple of days. If he was smart it was possible that he could use the situation to his advantage.

He did his best thinking in the morning, before the effects of wine fuddled his brain. A royal visit meant large crowds, and that meant, people who were more interested in watching what was happening than on their money.

A roguish grin spread across his face.

Jumping from the bed he ran to the old chest in his room where he stored his worn and rather meagre supply of tunics and sandals. He'd kept one tunic, just one, in case he ever needed it to attend an important occasion, and this was definitely it! Lifting it from the drawer he held it up to study it, pleased to find that it was just as he remembered – pristine white, well almost, and not a stain on it. He'd mix well with the crowd without ever being noticed.

The slovenly inn in which Varus lived stood in Vicolo di Frontone, close to the Nola Gate. For the most part the neighbourhood was a rabbit warren of narrow, grimy laneways which were unsafe after dark. But that was not where Varus intended to operate in a couple of days from now. He'd be around the major public areas such as the forum or lining the footpaths in places such as Via del Vesuvio.

Varus was a skilled pickpocket. He rubbed his hands with glee. The value of the coins, watches, bracelets and brooches, as well as many other items such as rings and purses that he expected to steal, would make life much more comfortable in the weeks ahead.

Estate of Julia Felix
Via dell'Abbondanza

At the far end of Via dell'Abbondanza, close to the amphitheatre, was the expansive estate of an intelligent and enterprising woman by the name of Julia Felix. She sat in her study working out how much extra money this coming official visit by the Empress would bring into her business.

She calculated that many visitors from the nearby towns such as Stabiae, Cumae and Nuceria would visit Pompeii to see the Empress. Julia offered services that she was sure would be in high demand.

Her villa and gardens covered nearly one whole block of land. Some was taken up by the villa itself, which was lavish and for her own private use. Also private, was the inner peristyle garden and the waterfall that beautified the area. In one corner stood a lararium, if she occasionally decided to pray to the gods.

Then, there was the remainder, which was totally used for business to bring in income. Her clients' bathhouse, which was expensive in comparison with the bathhouses beside the Marine Gate and near the forum, was expensively decorated and meant only for her guests or wealthy citizens or visitors.

Clean and attractive rooms in her inn with their own desks and windows that looked out on either the street or garden were always in high demand. And, of course, when the time of the visit arrived, her street food which was good quality and served hot to customers would be popular.

'Cleandros! Could you come in, please.'

'Yes, Domina.' Her elderly business manager made his way to her office from where he was working nearby.

'Salve.' I'm happy with these accounts you've given me this morning. Hopefully, we will bring in plenty of profit. I see that you're expecting quite an increase while the visit of the Empress is here. Is there anything you can think of that we need to change or order that I haven't thought of?'

'My only concern was whether the vegetables from your garden would be sufficient for the increased food that will need to be prepared.' Cleandros waited for her response.

'Mmm, I do believe you may be right to be concerned about sufficient supply. Speak to the cook for me and just check that she is sure we'll have enough. Otherwise, we'll have to order in more from outside.'

Julia ran her establishment with scrupulous care. She was a wealthy woman and also very sensible. There was no man in her private life, and she was middle-aged, so probably that time had passed her by, but one never knew what the future would bring and she was happy ensuring that her business ventures flourished. She knew that if he could see her now her father would be proud of her success, and that meant everything to her.

House of Vibius
Via di Mercurio

Vibius was the most experienced scribe in all of Pompeii. He was also growing old. His house, located not far from that of the surgeon, was small, with a tiny office at the front open to the street. For many years he'd been suffering from aches and pains and loss of mobility. Sometimes, he'd visit the surgeon in Via Consolare and pay a small amount for a poppy potion which took away some of the pain as well as helping him to sleep.

No one in Pompeii received any assistance from the city except for handouts of bread. Vibius was desperate to keep working for as long as he could, especially, as he had little or no savings.

This was the best time for him to write as the sun streamed in through the open doorway. His eyes were not so good any more. He was thankful to receive the fee, a good one, offered to him by the Duumvir, to write the invitations for those honoured to attend the luncheon and dinner during the visit of the Empress. He remembered Poppy when she was very young and would come with a servant to deliver work from her father to him. She was a likeable little girl, courteous and even then, lovely to look at. Vibius decided that he'd try to catch a glimpse of her near the city gate when she arrived.

Vibius admitted to himself that he was lonely. He lived alone and knew that death could not be very far away. Tears came to his eyes as he remembered his wonderful wife, dead for many years and his son, killed by a mob of thugs in a street fight. Wiping the tears away, he resolved to enjoy this one coming day, the royal procession and the feeling of being part of a community. He'd worry about the future when he had to.

He sat in the most comfortable chair he owned and took sheets of parchment, ink and a stylus from the top of his old desk. The task would take him a long time. The list had many names on it and he absolutely had to finish by late today. He knew that as he drew near the finish of the task his old fingers would ache and he'd barely be able to hold the stylus, but it would be worth it.

He set to work, delighted that the fee he'd be given would keep him in food for quite some time. He blessed the Empress and wished her well.

House of Livia
The Cosmetics Shop
Via di Castricio

Across the road and down a little from the perfume shop stood the delightful shop of Livia. She lived upstairs on her own and conducted her business on the ground floor. The ladies of Pompeii always knew where to go when they needed to look their best for a special occasion.

The visit of Rome's Empress was one such time. There was space on the ground floor for several ladies to sit on chairs provided, and others could enjoy exploring the wall shelves to find items such as hand mirrors or cosmetics available for purchase. Those who could afford it, luxuriated in having Livia personally apply those cosmetics to their faces that would highlight their beauty.

Livia was so busy that she didn't have time to eat. She went from one lady to prepare the face of another, while her assistant sold stock off the shelves.

She began with applying a dusting of white lead powder to hide any blemishes. Then, she darkened their eyebrows with a paste made from black soot taken from lamps. The favourite shade for eyelids was gold saffron, liberally applied. The finishing touches were applications of red dye delicately applied to both cheeks and lips. None of her customers asked the price when making a booking with Livia, they simply assumed it would be expensive. And it was.

If a customer hadn't already done so, Livia would farewell each of them with the strong recommendation that they should buy exquisite perfume. They shouldn't spoil such perfection by using a cheap fragrance. She sent them across the road to the exotically scented shop of her friend, Drusilla, who sold them vials of expensive rose, lily or lemon perfume. Then, she returned the favour by strongly recommending to her own customers that they visit Livia's cosmetics shop.

Livia was beaming with her success. She'd worked so hard building up her business. Finally, she could refurbish her house, especially where she lived upstairs. Poppy's visit was much appreciated.

The forum

The Basilica was undergoing renovation. Since the great earthquake almost a decade before, it had received little attention even though it was the main administrative centre for the city. With the imminent arrival of Rome's Empress, an effort was being made to at least bring back some of its lost beauty. It was the venue of the official welcome dinner.

A team of painters were restoring the brilliant colours of the building's exterior. By the time they'd finished, it was almost unrecognisable. Inside, as soon as the repairs had been completed, they began to repaint the walls. It took some time as the building was large with a raised dais at one end. Everyone's spirits lifted at the sight of the fresh, appealing colours. Soon, the organisers would come in with long tables to begin setting them up.

When Flaccus, the Duumvir, checked on progress late that afternoon, he was pleasantly surprised to find that everything was on schedule and his anxiety level began to fall. He walked the streets for one, final time and could find no fault.

Pompeii had never looked better.

Villa of Diomedes
Outside the Herculaneum Gate

'Statius, bring the horses around will you, we need to get going now before the heat rises.' Senator Lucius Diomedes decided that he'd personally visit Nuceria to arrange for praetorian support for the forthcoming visit of the Empress. The commander of the barracks would need sufficient time to re-allocate his troopers.

The day was warm and still as the handcarts of the farmers and other vendors arrived through the Herculaneum Gate on their way to the forum. The noise that announced their arrival was soon left behind as Lucius and his freedman, Statius, rode through the Nuceria Gate on the other side of Pompeii, and continued forward on the main road to Nuceria.

'You remembered the water?' Lucius glanced around him at the tombs lining the road on which they rode. It wasn't the most uplifting of sights.

'Yes, Senator.'

'Good. We should be able to reach the barracks without any delays. It's actually a pleasant enough journey, don't you think, on a day like this one?'

'It's quiet countryside, that's for sure,' Statius replied, 'it's been much better since the barracks was built. At least that stopped the robberies taking place along the roadside.'

They continued on for some time in silence and it wasn't long before the first signs of the town could be seen in the distance. An amphitheatre welcomed them and a little further on, a theatre.

Daughter of Pompeii

They passed through the town centre and on the far side came to the praetorian barracks. It was a relatively recent construction and in very good condition.

'What is your business?' one of the entry guards asked.

'Senator Lucius Diomedes from Pompeii requests a few words with commander Valentius.'

The guard checked them for weapons then waved them through. Lucius was pleased to find himself welcomed almost immediately into the presence of commander Albertus Valentius.

'What brings you to see me today, Senator?' Valentius enquired mildly as he carried two cups of wine to his desk and handed one to his visitor.

'Security,' Lucius sat back comfortably in his chair.

'For what area?'

'As you may know, the Empress is visiting Pompeii. I've discussed this matter with the Duumvir, and we're both concerned that enough security should be provided to guarantee her safety and prevent, as far as possible, additional problems in the streets. I've come to ask if you would be prepared to allocate additional troopers for that particular day in Pompeii.'

'Actually, trooper Capito alerted me to the event. But as you seem somewhat concerned, perhaps we should provide more than just a watchful couple of troopers. I'll be pleased to help you, Senator. On that day the praetorian presence will be obvious. It should prove a deterrent to anyone seeking to disturb the celebrations.'

With mutual good wishes expressed between the two men, they parted having successfully concluded a firm arrangement.

On their arrival back in Pompeii, Lucius stopped in at the Basilica where he spoke with Aeneus. 'Well, between us we've done all we can,' Lucius told him as they sat talking in Aeneus' office.

'Yes. I don't think anyone's expecting any problems but you never know, and the Empress is too important to be placed at any risk,' Aeneus accompanied Lucius to the door of the building.

'I'm sure everything will work out well!' Lucius said reassuringly as he left him standing on the steps and made his way back to his villa. He found himself unexpectedly quite looking forward to the visit. There hadn't been anything much for the people to enjoy since the destruction caused by the savage earthquake some years ago.

27

Inn of the Sulpicii
(On the fringe of Pompeii)

Blazing torches, their flames dancing like liquid gold slithered through the blackness of the night, embracing Poppy's carriage emblazoned with the royal emblem as it approached the inn. It turned into the circular drive and crunched to a stop. Poppy was assisted down from the carriage by one of the owners who'd been watching for her arrival.

'Welcome. It is an honour to have you at our establishment,' Cornelius Sulpicius said, bowing low.

'Thank you.'

Poppy turned to the praetorians who had escorted her, and sat unmoving on their horses which had begun to snort and grow restless.

'My thanks for your protection. I will be glad of your service again for my visit to the city. Good night.'

The praetorian in charge inclined his head in recognition of her words and the small group followed a groom to an adjacent building.

Poppy was so tired that she barely noticed the interior of the exquisite jewel of a villa, well lit and shining, as she was escorted through the ample reception area and into the wide, central hallway. Large, vivid frescoes featuring colours of red and green were painted on the walls. To each side, the hallway doors, presently closed, were suites with their own bathing facilities. In all, there were five.

Right at the end of the hallway the huge, master suite lay positioned crossways to the hall, with a double, heavy door leading inside. As it was opened, Poppy was pleased to see a large, comfortable bed prepared for her use and a small bathing area in the adjacent room.

'Is there anything else you require, Empress?' Cornelius asked helpfully.

'Please send a maid to assist me. Also, I know it's late but do you by any chance have hot food available?'

'We anticipated that you would need refreshment. We can offer you fish with garum sauce, or perhaps, you'd prefer starlings' wings in honey?'

'Thank you. I'd prefer the fish.'

The owner left her and hurried away to arrange her request. No sooner had she'd bathed and dressed for bed than the food was ready and she ate it gratefully before falling into the bed. It took only minutes for her to descend into a deep and dreamless sleep.

The villa was completely silent as the owners had ensured that there were no other occupants. Poppy slept late the next morning and the sunshine was bright when she eventually rose and opened the door at the back of her suite leading into the garden.

She was surprised to see that the villa overlooked the city as it stood on higher ground, so she was able to look down over the honey coloured roofs. There was no sound except for the twittering of the birds. As requested, she ordered breakfast and ate it as she enjoyed the solitude.

Today was a special pleasure. It was a day of rest.

The next day, refreshed and looking forward to her visit home, Poppy woke early to allow plenty of time to dress with the aid of a maid. With her hair and make up complete, she looked every inch an empress. She sat quietly for a few minutes thinking about the event. She'd left as a young woman, innocent and naïve, she'd return as the Empress of the Roman Empire.

It had been a long journey upwards. She sat pondering if, in the end, it had all been worth it. There was no doubt, however, that even now her mind still held onto the revenge that burned within. When would her achievements ever be enough for her to gain inner peace?

Regardless, for Poppy, this was a day of triumph.

Having profusely thanked the owner of the inn she stepped outside and into her coach. The praetorian guards filed out to either side and they commenced the short journey into the heart of Pompeii.

The day of Poppy's official visit to Pompeii arrived cool and crisp and Farzana worried all morning about whether she'd found her night at the inn acceptable. The whole family, with the exception of Aeneus, walked to Via del Vesuvio early, to find a good place from which to watch the procession. He was on duty on horseback closer to the forum.

Pompeii looked its best except, perhaps, for the repairs still not fully completed since the great earthquake. Before long, Poppy's carriage arrived through the Vesuvius Gate, the horses travelling at a gentle pace so that people would have an opportunity to see her.

For just a moment, as she passed, Poppy saw Farzana and as their eyes met, looked straight at her as she waved.

'She saw you,' Aulus said, excitedly to Farzana.

'I know. I think she looks absolutely like an empress, and so beautiful.'

An official welcome was held in the forum. During the speeches, Varus mingled, unnoticed, with the crowd. He stole as much as possible and by the time he returned to his room that afternoon, the bag was full.

He was extremely thankful to the Empress.

Poppy took a short walk through part of the city with Clodius Flaccus, the Duumvir, and several chosen city councillors. She smiled slightly, glancing at the bench that she and Farzana considered their own in the garden at the Temple of Venus as they walked past. She'd particularly asked to return to her home and on reaching it, found herself emotional as she stood overwhelmed, remembering the terrible day that she'd last been there. She declined an invitation to step inside.

An intimate lunch was provided for Poppy which was held at the House of Sallust Hospitium in Via Consolare. This stately private house which had been turned into a hotel, included rooms for travellers as well as private apartments usually rented by residents.

As they entered the Hospitium, Flaccus nodded to the porter standing at his post in front of the entry to the private apartments. He stepped aside to allow the Duumvir and his royal guest as well as the others to enter the prearranged apartment for lunch.

Comfortably seated, Poppy conversed easily with the city's selected guests. She realised that she hadn't kept herself informed as much as she should have about the state of Pompeii's various communities.

'Is the city still producing a large amount of wine to send to other parts of the Empire?' she asked the city's most prosperous banker, Caecilius Jucundus.

'Yes, Empress. It remains very popular. In fact, Vesuviano wine will be served at the reception this evening.'

She turned to speak to Umbricius Scaurus, owner of the business which supplied the best quality garum fish sauce in the Empire. 'And your fish sauce business continues to thrive, Umbricius?'

'We cannot make enough of it to supply all of the requests.'

'I'll consider myself fortunate, then. For it is used in my own kitchens at the palace,' Poppy laughed. 'I cannot tell you how happy I am to be able to return home to Pompeii. I shall always treasure this visit.'

Poppy was given use of the apartment for her personal needs after the lunch until the evening, when it would be time for the official dinner. It was a pleasant place, looking out on a pretty garden peristyle.

Farzana, Aulus and Marcellus and his wife were seated at the same table with Poppy that evening. Aeneus, still in uniform, stood watching by the side door. The dinner went well. There was a relaxed atmosphere, especially following an excellent speech by Senator Diomedes.

At the conclusion, when Poppy left, it was to travel the short distance through the city gate to her own villa, ready and waiting for her at Oplontis.

28

Villa of Oplontis
The Next Morning

Farzana arrived at Poppy's villa ready for her stay. She was pleased that there would be time together for the two of them. It had been a while since that had been possible. She knocked on the door and Poppy came herself to open it.

'Finally, we'll have time to talk together,' she said, laughing, as the two women embraced then walked arm in arm into the atrium. The perfume of roses was everywhere.

'Everything is perfect. Thank you so much, Farzana.'

'I'm pleased that you like it, Poppy, I hope I chose the right cubiculum for you?'

'It's absolutely perfect. Now, I have something to suggest to you.' Poppy drew Farzana down onto the couch with her. 'Do you think that if you asked your father, Marcellus and Aeliana, as well as Aeneus, of course, that they would all come to dinner here with us tomorrow night.'

'I'm sure they'd be thrilled.'

'Give me a moment, then,' Poppy said, jumping up, 'and I'll get a messenger.'

A few minutes later she returned. 'That's done. Now comes the difficult part,' her expression was serious. Then, she began to laugh, 'we must choose the menu so that cook can arrange for the food and, of course, prepare it.'

They sat giggling like young girls as they decided, then changed their minds, and finally did decide on what they'd like prepared for dinner.

Poppy rang a tiny silver bell and when the maid appeared, gave her the list to take straight to the kitchen.

She turned to Farzana and this time her serious expression did not change.

'Farzana, where will you live when you marry Aeneus?' she asked.

'Father has said that his house will become ours, but he will live there and one of the bedrooms will be his while he lives.'

'That is a firm decision is it?'

'Yes.'

Poppy was silent and appeared lost in thought. She broke the silence and asked Farzana, 'Would you please let me give you an early wedding present?'

'You know your friendship is gift enough,' Farzana replied softly.

'You're precious to me. You are my sister.' Poppy had tears in her eyes. 'I ask in no way in disrespect, but I know that your family are not wealthy people, and they've all worked so hard. I love your charming house, but would you let me send in the painters, mosaic floor workmen, and gardeners to restore it to the home I'd like you to have. You deserve it!'

Farzana sat speechless.

'Please tell me I haven't offended you,' Poppy said as she watched her anxiously, 'but I'd like to give you something that will make a real difference to your life.'

Farzana drew closer and embraced Poppy.

'I don't know how to thank you.' Tears ran down Farzana's cheeks and soon they were both half-crying and half-laughing.

They spent the remainder of the day enjoying the huge pool in the garden. As dusk approached, they sat at the top of the cliff watching a blood-red sun sink lower and lower below the horizon, turning the sky pink, as day became night.

Farzana awoke next morning looking forward to the day ahead. She heard Poppy calling her. When she followed the sound until she reached her, Farzana found Poppy luxuriating in a milk bath with dozens of rose petals floating in it.

'You're welcome to join me,' Poppy offered.

Farzana laughed. 'It's not quite what I'm used to, so I'll leave it to you, at least for now,' she declined.

'As you wish, but it's one of my favourite luxuries.'

A little later, Poppy emerged from her rooms dressed for the day and the two sat down to breakfast. She became emotional as she began to discuss her life.

'There are times now when I have the uncomfortable feeling that time is running out for me, and it's too late now to change my life. I'm married to a man who is becoming increasingly unstable and dangerous, and I've done things that would not make you proud of me.'

'You shouldn't take all of the blame,' Farzana interrupted. 'You've done what you have for a reason, and what you were subjected to when you were very young was evil and devastating.' When she looked across at her, she realised that Poppy was more upset than she'd ever seen her before.

'I'm lonely, Farzana. Regardless of all of the people around me, they are simply passing through my life. I spend limited time with my son and hide him away, because Nero has become someone I cannot trust with Rufrius. I live in fear for both of us.'

Poppy began to sob as Farzana held her, feeling helpless to offer any solutions. She wept as if her heart would break and it was some time before she quieted. Farzana could see how distraught Poppy was and realised that her own efforts at reassurance were little more than hollow gestures.

'Let's go into the garden,' she suggested. Together they walked slowly outside and sat down beneath the plane tree. They sat there for some time.

'Do you believe in destiny?' Farzana finally asked.

'I'm not sure I've really given that very much thought, Poppy replied.'

'Poppy, I know you as generous, warm and loyal. There may be things you've done that come from other parts of your nature, but I will always know you as I have done ever since that first day in the forum. You've obviously reached a very difficult time in your life. Be careful, be wise and look after yourself and your son. Most of all, try to be as happy as you can and don't be so hard on yourself. That's best left to others.'

Poppy was back to her usual self by the time the day had passed and with the arrival of night, the flares and candles were lit once more. The aroma of delicious food told them that dinner was not far away.

'Aeneus, you're here!' Farzana called as the maid opened the door to admit him. He was soon followed by Aulus, Marcellus and Aeliana. The introductions made, they sat down to wine and tiny, pre-dinner exotic dishes.

Farzana saw that Poppy took the opportunity to draw Aulus aside. For several minutes they conversed with lowered voices. She watched him begin with a neutral look on his face which rapidly changed to one of surprise and then delight. It wasn't difficult to guess that Poppy had asked for his permission to make the changes to the house that she'd offered Farzana.

Later, Farzana would look back on that evening as one of the most memorable pleasures she'd had in her life. It was a warm memory full of love, friendship and laughter in a setting of great beauty.

'Hinnulus,' his assistant called, 'there's a messenger here with a message for you.'

'Just take it,' he yelled back impatiently.

'I really think you should come yourself.'

Hinnulus threw down his brush impatiently. Why did he have to do everything himself? This, however, was no ordinary messenger. The message requested his presence at the Oplontis villa tomorrow afternoon to discuss future work.

'I was told to return with an answer.'

'The answer is *yes*,' Hinnulus said. After the messenger had gone, he scratched his head as to what the additional work could be. The Empress expected only the best, but she also paid well. He returned to his task happy with the world.

'I *told* you!' his son commented cheekily.

'Just mind your own business,' Hinnulus answered with mock severity, or one day your attitude will get you into a lot of trouble.'

First, Hinnulus turned up at the villa where he was told exactly what was required with painting and wall mosaics. He was surprised that this work was to be done at one of the ordinary houses in Pompeii. Wisely, he kept his questions to himself.

Next, came the mosaic layer who had completed the work on the Oplontis villa's floors. He took detailed notes as to what Poppy thought might look best in the house. Then, she spoke with the senior gardener who was presently there pruning and generally tidying up the garden.

Finally, she requested a visit from Clodius Flaccus, the Duumvir. When he arrived, she spoke quietly with him for several minutes then handed him documents previously prepared in Rome.

Poppy felt very pleased with herself when the arrangements for the work she wanted done had finally been concluded. She'd been very careful that her wishes were clear, so there was no reason to think that any problems would follow. It lowered her anxiety considerably. She was someone who took great joy from giving to those close to her.

The work on the house of Aulus was completed just before Poppy returned to Rome. The changes she'd requested were all done and the house looked like it belonged to someone else, someone very well off. None of the family could help themselves just standing and staring at it for long periods of time, until they became used to the fact that it actually belonged to them. They were enchanted by it.

The garden had been totally replanted and a lovely, gurgling fountain stood at its centre. A new birdbath and bench had also been brought in.

The house had been painted inside with magnificent wall frescoes added, and a bright kitchen fitted with new dishes and drinking cups supplied as well as other utensils. The floor mosaics, laid with intricate detail and care, were of the highest quality and new beds and linens had also been supplied.

Expensive floor and wall lamps added to the feeling of luxury but it was Aulus who was overcome the most, when he saw his new front work bench and shop area. It had been totally replaced with expensive fittings as well as a comfortable chair for use by customers.

The most surprising difference, however, was a tiny sitting room added in the small space available at the side of the house. It wasn't large, but very comfortably furnished with beautiful fittings. On the wall, Poppy had ordered a fresco of Venus holding a child. It was the perfect place for one of them to go for peace and reading or just sitting, because the house was small and there had been no other space for any of them before, to escape for a few private moments.

They blessed Poppy for her friendship and caring. All of them felt the huge difference in the quality of their lives.
Hinnulus had spent many hours painting the new frescoes and friezes in the house of Aulus. The work was finished, except for one last remaining feature. He'd removed nearly all of his buckets and brushes from the house prior to the recent wedding. He was pleased with the finished job, which had utterly changed the appearance of the interior.

One morning, when Hinnulus had the house to himself to do a few last minute "touch-ups," he kept his word to Poppy. Checking to ensure he was alone, he faced the wall where he'd painted a lovely, outdoor scene. A few roses remained to be completed on the bottom, right hand side of the fresco as well as a couple of poppies. Behind one of them he hid a message. It could be revealed by carefully removing part of the roses. That is, if someone knew it was there.

Aeneus and Farzana were married in the lovely garden at the back of their stunning new house. A few friends attended with the family, and when Duumvir, Clodius Flaccus heard about the ceremony he attended out of respect for Poppy.

The sun rose in a blue sky with a few cotton wool clouds on a warm day with a slight breeze. The couple were so obviously in love that the marriage brought joy to all who saw them. They returned to Stabiae to celebrate the beginning of their lives together in one of the villas on the clifftop looking out across the sea.

They were so close to Vesuvius that they needed only to look up to realise that they were standing in its shadow.

Aeneus Capito had been born in Napoli. The son of parents of comfortable but not wealthy means, his was a large family.

Daughter of Pompeii

From the time he'd been very young he'd been drawn to the praetorians on patrol in the city.

It was no surprise when he informed his parents that he intended to enlist, but they were not quite so happy when he was sent to the south to the barracks at Nuceria, where he served for several years.

There was something about Farzana that drew him to her. He was never quite sure whether it was her gentle nature or her spontaneous laughter, but he did know that he'd fallen in love with her, and it was inevitable that they'd marry.

The situation with Poppy, the refurbishment of what Aulus referred to as "their home" and the magnificence of the villa at Oplontis had all come as unexpected shocks, even if pleasant ones. Aeneus did have one problem, about which he said little to Farzana so as not to worry her. He wondered what type of work he could get now he'd had to leave the praetorians.

Unknown to Aeneus, fate had one surprise left for him. On returning from their holiday to Stabiae after their marriage, he was called to the office of Duumvir, Clodius Flaccus. He was surprised but not unduly worried.

'Salve Aeneus. Do come in. It's a pleasure to see you. I trust you and Farzana enjoyed your time in Stabiae? It was, indeed a lovely wedding,' Clodius greeted him. 'Please sit.'

After further pleasant conversation and an offer of wine which Aeneus declined, Clodius came to the reason for the present meeting. Aeneus watched him expectantly.

'It's my pleasure to offer you a position as my assistant here at the Basilica. If you think you might be interested, I can give you detailed information about the duties involved. They are not difficult, but I do need someone who can be trusted with confidential documents and is of trustworthy character. What do you think?'

'I think that this may be exactly what I would like, especially as I have just resigned from the Guard,' Aeneus answered.

'The Empress spoke to me for some time when she was here,' Clodius informed him. 'It so happens that by the time she left, I found myself with a position I needed to fill. I can assure you, in case you're wondering, that this is an additionally created position, not one vacated by anyone else's departure.'

'Poppy,' Aeneus shook his head, incredulity in his voice, 'we owe her so much.'

'Our empress is indeed special,' Clodius complimented her, 'and I'm pleased to offer you the position. Will you accept?'

'I will. And, thank you.'

I've had a list of duties drawn up in expectation that you might agree,' Clodius added and handed it to Aeneus. 'You will commence, if it's suitable to you, in one week.'

Aeneus left the Basilica feeling very fortunate, which he was. He hurried back to the house to give Farzana the good news.

'It sounds like Poppy was even more busy when she was here than we ever knew,' she commented thoughtfully. 'Surely, there can't be anything else she didn't tell us.'

'She's a lady of incredible generosity,' Aeneus praised her, 'we are truly blessed by the gods to have her friendship. There is no way we can ever repay her.'

The gods smiled with amusement as they kept their secret.

29

ROME

Poppy immediately noticed the difference in Rome when she returned. The new work that had been carried out on the Golden Palace and surrounding parkland and lake since she'd been away was well advanced with only some finishing touches to be completed. Nero was still in Portus and his return was not expected for some time but there had been word of how much effort he was giving to the practices.

'The Golden Palace is finished enough for you to move into your apartment,' Severus informed her a few days after her return. 'If you wish, myself and Celer can give you a tour of the palace,' he offered. 'It really is special.'

Poppy accepted with pleasure. 'I would certainly like to see it. Please allow the artists to keep working when I come, I'd be interested to watch them. I'll have time tomorrow afternoon.'

On her way to her apartment she called in to see her son. Rufrius was playing a noisy game of soldiers with Tigellinus who was down on his knees. Poppy smiled to herself. Very few had seen the commander of the praetorians in such a position. He'd obviously become a surrogate father to the little boy.

For a moment or two her presence wasn't noticed until Rufrius looked up and saw her.

'Mother, Tigi and I are playing war!'

'What a wonderful game!' Poppy answered, gathering him in her arms. 'You are a lucky boy to have a real soldier like Tigi to play with.' She hadn't missed the affectionate, shortened from of Tigellinus' name her son used.

Tigellinus got to his feet not in the least embarrassed.

'Empress, I believe we may have a future praetorian here,' he laughed. 'Welcome back.'

'I can't thank you enough for what you're doing for Rufrius. A boy needs a man's influence. Tigellinus, if ever you should need a favour....' Poppy didn't finish, leaving it up to him to understand the offer.

'My thanks to you, empress. One never knows. Now I should leave.'

After he'd gone, Poppy spent time playing with her son then handed him over to the care of the maid. Even with all that had been on her mind when she was away, she'd missed her young son. She worried about his future if ever something should happen to her. The world she lived in was dangerous and uncertain.

Over the weeks that followed rumours reached her of trouble with several senators. Helius became more and more agitated and discussed the situation with her.

They agreed that they would try to entice Nero to return to Rome, then wait a little before he journeyed to Greece to see if the situation stabilised.

Daughter of Pompeii

One morning Poppy walked to the Forum with a praetorian guard for safety. She lingered for a time, watching the hawkers selling their flapping chickens and a slave sale taking place nearby. Beggars lounged around the steps of temples and small groups of men stood talking. Here and there senators could be seen heading for the curia, and advocates pushed their way through the crowds to the courthouse.

Litters with their curtains closed made their way through, heading for other destinations, and those intent on financial affairs passed through the Forum on the way to the nearby banks. It was a scene of noise and vitality.

Poppy asked for admission at the entry to the house of the vestals, adjacent to the temple where a flame was always kept burning. It wasn't long before she was granted a private meeting with the senior vestal.

'Salve. How may I help you?' she asked.

Poppy handed her documents. 'This is my will. To prevent any misunderstanding later, please witness this now. The vestal perused it then added her signature.

'Do you wish me to hold this securely here?' the vestal asked.

'Here, I believe, is the safest place for it to be kept,' Poppy agreed as the vestal nodded.

'Is there anything else you wish to leave with me?'

'No. That is all.' Poppy answered.

'Be assured your will is safe.'

The vestal placed a reassuring hand on her arm and offered refreshments, which Poppy declined. She looked around her and noticed the beautiful garden that was part of the vestals' complex.

'Would you like to walk with me in the garden?' the vestal suggested. 'We're most fortunate to have such beautiful surroundings in which to live.'

Poppy rose from her chair and together they strolled amongst the flowers and fountains. They spoke of general well-being and the future of Rome.

'Your garden reminds me of home in Pompeii. I think it's because of the roses,' Poppy commented. 'Thank you for your advice and your hospitality. I must leave you now and return to so many things that need attention.'

The vestal turned and lowered her voice. 'Empress, you have a shadow hanging over you. Are you aware of that?'

'I have been aware of it for some time,' Poppy sighed. 'Do you have any advice for me?'

The vestal's face betrayed her sadness. 'Try to be at peace, only the gods can decide your destiny.'

Poppy departed with a heavy heart but she also felt relief that her will was safe. There was nothing more she could do. She would look after the people dear to her and as to the future, she must let destiny fall where it may.

30

The Domus Aurea
(The Golden Palace)

She felt so very, very small!

Poppy gasped as she stood just inside the main entrance to the Domus Aurea. The approach had been through long, seemingly never-ending colonnades of African marble columns and mother of pearl, gems and gold studded walls, stunning as they shone a brilliant gold in the sunshine.

And still, they did not prepare the visitor for the wonder of what lay within.

Visitors would arrive on one of two main roads that ran through the Palatine to the main entry and buildings of the new palace. The surrounding gardens had been restored to their former beauty before the ravages of the fire.

Poppy arched her neck back as far as she could to stare at the ceilings that welcomed her inside as they soared skywards.

She felt totally insignificant in this space. Speechless, she moved further inside to begin her tour with Severus. She turned to him, but was unable to utter a word so she simply walked on. Little did she know that the palace would increase in sophistication and wonder the further she progressed.

Colour, colour everywhere rich and exquisite!

Fabulus, the famous Roman fresco painter, as well as others of distinction, had painted masterpieces on the walls so vibrant and gorgeous that they had an opulence that defied description. They were classical in nature, frisky or so delicate, especially the friezes, that the brushwork seemed to have simply danced across the walls like a butterfly. They stunned the viewer in expensive blues, reds and gold.

Poppy stopped to speak with a young woman who was finishing a frieze. The ceiling above had already been painted.

'What wonderful artistry you have,' Poppy complimented her.

'It's such a pleasure to have this opportunity,' she answered, holding the brush delicately in her hand. 'So many of us have work now where before this, we had hardly any.'

'Your name is Hortensia, is it not?' Severus asked.

'It is. I'm so glad you both like my painting.'

Poppy walked on and the girl returned to her task, humming as she did so.

'I should tell you, empress, there are hundreds of rooms in this palace,' Severus informed her. 'It would be very easy to become lost here.'

'Then we should walk just a little quicker,' Poppy laughed. She stopped to stare at a magnificent statue of a goddess placed in the central aisle of the hallway.' She stood in wonder gazing at her red-coloured hair and the gold that trimmed her white robe. She wondered, but did not ask, if there were echoes of herself in the beautiful woman she was studying. Are there other statues this wonderful?' she asked Severus.

'Empress, there are over five hundred statues in total. I see you look sceptical. A large number of these were "borrowed" shall we say, from Delphi.'

Poppy was unsure if that was a good thing or not, so she simply accepted it. As they continued on, she became aware of a change in the decoration of the hallways and rooms where they walked. The amount and quality of marble around them and under their feet began to change. There was more of it and marble of different colour had been used such as opulent green marble from Spartica.

The bedrooms they had seen were splendid, but as they moved further into the interior, she saw others even more ornate. They had lattice-work ceilings from which fell perfume and petals. The smell of incense infused the air as well as fragranced oil from intricate oil lamps.

As they reached the Octagonal Room, Severus glanced at Poppy to gauge her reaction. At the top of the domed ceiling was an ocular opening so that light spilled inside.

The room's roof revolved day and night and perfume and flower petals could be released to gently drift down upon those below.

'This is absolutely dazzling!' Poppy declared with awe.

'I believe that was the Emperor's intention,' Severus smiled. 'I hope it will please him.'

The room was a huge space with four large alcoves decorated with statues, and couches looking inwards. On the walls, exquisite fresco panels drew the gaze of any visitor, and it was impossible not to feel overwhelmed by the sheer size of the space.

It was, however, the sight and sound of the oversized waterfall that cascaded over a marble wall from an unbelievable height, only to fall like thunder into a pool below, that provided the most impact. Droplets of water caught the natural light and that from oil lamps, as they splashed from the impact caused by the fall to the floor below.

The effect was relaxation and coolness that flowed throughout the room.

'What is the purpose of this room,' Poppy asked, 'apart from achieving a dazzling impact and an impression of power and beauty?'

'This room can be used for a number of occasions. It could be for groups dining here, for purely business transactions or perhaps, for musical, and poetry recitals or other entertainments as the Emperor wished. I believe it is quite flexible.'

Severus glanced at Poppy. 'If I may beg a favour, empress?'

'Certainly, Severus,' Poppy answered somewhat puzzled.

'If you'll allow me, I should like to be the one to show you your first look at the apartment especially designed for you.'

A look of pleasure crossed her face as she gestured to him to move on. Solid double doors stood open to reveal a sweeping marble floor throughout an apartment consisting of an entry reception, sitting room, dining alcove, main bedroom, second bedroom and bathing area.

The back of Poppy's apartment opened out to a private, covered portico with the water of a pretty lagoon pool, separated from the lake, lapping against it. High bamboo and palm branches overhung this totally private area on both sides, providing shade from the sun. At its centre, the pool featured four smaller fountains that gurgled and splashed. The sound and sight of the water in such a setting was both relaxing and inspiring.

Poppy sat down in one of the chairs provided, a look of serenity on her face. 'This, is what I've always wanted. Thank you, Severus, your design is perfect!'

'Then, it has been worth all of the work,' he bowed to her.

'I can't say it's been easy, but it's a remarkable palace!'

She rose to go, wishing she didn't have to. But she'd be back here soon. They left the apartment and walked on through one of the hallways.

'We've come to a side exit here, would you like to go through to the gardens?' Severus suggested. He'd been extremely pleased, though not totally surprised by Poppy's reaction to the palace, especially her apartment, but he would have been disappointed not to have her see the outside attractions.

'The gardens and terraces are built on the Caelian Hill,' he explained as they went out into the sunshine. 'The area is so large that we have included features such as the intricate fountains some of which you can see from here and also woodland and cornfields.

The centrepiece is the large man-made lake. The fountain, as you can see, is presently being installed and will be magnificent once it is functioning. Indeed, it is in itself, a work of art.'

The basic, temporary huts of workers were spread across the fringes of the gardens. They were provided with this free accommodation as well as their food.

'Empress, do you see that area where the workmen are today?'

'Yes, what is it?'

'They're building very strong, fortified enclosures for the animals that will be arriving here very soon. Many of them are coming from Africa but animals from other places will also be featured. I'm sure people will be enthralled when they see them.'

Continuing their walk she wasn't sure whether to feel awed or afraid by the colossal bronze statue of Nero presently being lifted into place. An emperor so much larger than his people was surely a risk.

Poppy moved into her new apartment within a week. It was exquisitely furnished and fully completed. Her son, Rufrius' much smaller apartment was finished and located next door. During this period of Nero's extended absence Poppy had more private time than usual.

She sat pondering how Nero could be veering towards insanity much of the time, but even though he'd begun to plan this new palace several years ago, before he'd descended quite so far from normality, this palace was proof of its owner's artistic vision and love of beauty. She was sure he'd also planned it not only for personal pleasure, but also to showcase his power. That was understandable. The question in her mind, however, was had he gone too far?

Poppy shook her head. She couldn't understand how the two things, creativity and madness, quite complemented each other. Rumours reached her that his enemies in the senate were circling.

Nero needed to return if he was to survive.

31

Portus
(The Port of Rome)

Nero's eyes glittered with feverish excitement as his retinue passed through Ostia and before long a large amphitheatre came into sight. It stood silhouetted against the skyline, a giant confirmation of Rome's skill and power. It was adjacent to Portus, the new port built by Claudius, astonishing in its own right.

'We're here! We're here!' Nero yelled with the excitement of a small child. 'Aelianus, when can we practise?'

The trainer groaned inwardly. It had been a long journey considering that they'd all had little rest and he was tired.

'The best time would be early tomorrow morning,' he suggested with as much enthusiasm in his voice as he could muster.

'Not until then?' the petulant expression those near him had all become so used to, appeared on Nero's face.

'Not until then!' Aelianus repeated firmly. 'You must not drive unless you are rested, if you do you will not be at your best.'

'You are right, of course,' Nero conceded. 'Only the best is acceptable for champions.'

The trainer nodded and sighing inwardly with relief, left to find out which tent he'd had allocated to him. If his job didn't bring so many benefits, he thought, it wouldn't be worth it. Then, he remembered the adoring looks of the women who thronged around the drivers, and also any of the trainers who were presentable. He grinned.

Hour after hour and day after day Nero practised. It went on and on until everyone around him was bored and exhausted. His level of energy seemed surreal.

As everyone knew it eventually had to, the day finally dawned when Nero declared himself ready to drive in the next festival in Rome. They could all pack up and go home. He was particularly pleased when the trainer told him that if they got back in time, he might just be able to watch the chariot races scheduled to take place in the Circus Maximus.

They arrived back in Rome on the morning of the races. Hurrying back to his palace, now the new golden palace, Nero barely glanced at it, much to the chagrin of Severus and Celer. He raced through the hallways until the attendant stopped at the door to his apartment.

That afternoon, Nero sat in the royal box at the Circus Maximus deep in concentration, as he watched the chariots racing around the central spina as one by one the dolphins fell to count each lap. He projected himself into the race, seeing himself as the eventual winner.

As the day wore on, he began to talk to a few of those around him. Suddenly, he flew into a violent rage and stalked out of the box and the stadium. Praetorian guards had to hustle to form around him as he walked fuelled by adrenaline towards the palace.

'Why did you lie to me?'

As dusk fell Nero burst into Poppy's apartment in a rage.

She turned to face him, surprised by the level of his fury. 'What do you mean?' she asked calmly. 'When did I lie to you?'

'Get out!' he yelled at the nearby slave. She fled quickly from the scene. Those just outside the room made themselves as invisible as possible.

Nero moved to stand closer to Poppy. Then he snarled at her. 'There are rumours openly circulating that it was *not* the Christians who started the fire. There are murmurings that I've killed innocent people. In the eyes of Rome's citizens that makes me a murderer!'

His fury was such that Nero could barely speak. Stepping forward, he shook her violently by the shoulders.

'Stop. You're hurting me!' Poppy yelled as she tried to escape his grip.

'You're a Jewess. But you're not a Christian are you!' he shouted. 'I'm told that the two groups hate each other. It never occurred to me when you told me you were sure the Christians had done it, that you'd purposely lie to me in order to divert attention away from the Jews.'

'Many senators as well as some of the people actually think that *you* started the fire.' Poppy's patience snapped and she sneered at him. 'They don't respect you and you know it! What else can you expect when you run around entertaining on stages in theatres and driving chariots in public races?'

Nero hit her with the full force of a blow that knocked her to the floor, her head striking a side table on the way down.

She lay there like a broken doll.

'You're a liar! The people love me on stage and at the Circus!' Nero screamed at her, his face ravaged by fury.

There was no answer from Poppy.

As Tigellinus and other praetorians entered the room, Nero began to kick Poppy who was heavily pregnant. They were horrified to see sticky, crimson blood begin to seep out around her as her body lay motionless.

Yells for help brought the servants running. They took in the scene with disbelief and chaos broke out. Any attempt to revive her failed.

The Empress of Rome was dead.

Nero stood staring until they pulled him away from her. The praetorians forcibly removed him from the room and took him to his apartment, where he was left locked inside, with guards outside to prevent him exiting back through the door.

An expression of sadness crossed Tigellinus' face as he gazed down at Poppy. Gently, he lifted up her head. She had her faults, but for all that, he'd really liked her. He'd always been loyal to this emperor he served, but not for much longer. Tigellinus would continue his duty, but should Nero fall into further disrepute by his own actions, the praetorian commander would not be there to save him.

32

One Morning Several Weeks Later

Nero sat perfectly still, staring vacantly in front of him. He'd been in that position for some time. Suddenly, he jumped to his feet looking disoriented. 'Tigellinus!' he roared suddenly.

The Prefect walked quickly into the room. 'You wish to speak to me Caesar?'

'There you are! I want you to kill him.'

'Who?'

'The child, Rufrius Crispinus, of course.'

Tigellinus' face turned pale. 'Are you sure?'

'Yes, I'm sure. Make it look like an accident.'

'Like the last boating accident?' Tigellinus asked, his voice betraying nothing. His veiled reference to the murder of Nero's mother, Agrippina, passed by Nero unnoticed.

'He distresses me,' Nero whimpered. 'I have no child of my own. I can't stand to see him near me.' His eyes filled with self-pitying tears. 'He's a nuisance. I wish to marry again and I can't have that boy wandering around.'

Tigellinus waited in silence to be dismissed.

'Kill the other one too. Kill his father.'

'I regret, Caesar, that I cannot.'

'Why? Are you refusing to carry out my orders?' Nero's face turned an ugly shade of purple.

Tigellinus frowned. 'Because he's already long dead by the order of Messalina.'

'Oh.' Nero's face took on a crumpled appearance as he sank down and reclined once more.

'Will that be all, Caesar?'

'It should have been *my* son that Poppy carried, not that fool, Crispinus!' Nero began to ramble.

Tigellinus turned on his heel and left the room.

He strode rapidly through the palace looking for the only man whose friendship was absolutely unbreakable, his second in command, Marcus. He saw him as he was about to enter through one of the doors leading from the garden.

'Marcus, come with me!'

'But where....'

'I'll explain everything in a few moments but we must be quick.'

Almost at a run, Tigellinus and Marcus made their way to Rufrius' apartment. Relief flooded through Tigellinus as he caught sight of the boy, uninjured.

'Tigi!'

'It's only me, Rufrius.' He took the boy's hand as he lifted him up.

'It's not enough, Marcus, that Nero's murdered his wife, but now he's ordered that I kill her innocent son. I cannot do it! I have a plan that may allow the boy to escape, but I need help to fabricate his death. Are you with me?'

'Of course. This emperor's days are numbered, he's close to complete madness now.'

'I thought you might say that.'

'Tell me your plan.'

The Campania Coastline
(South of Baiae)

Later that night, one conspicuous for the lack of any moonlight or activity nearby, Tigellinus and Marcus lifted the body of a boy with dark hair into a small boat. It bobbed about on gentle waves. Wading into the dark water they climbed into it and began rowing out to deeper water.

The body was then dumped overboard.

It hit the sea with a splash and quickly sank.

Neither man had time to mourn the death of the unknown boy who'd been chosen from others who'd just died in the narrow laneways of Rome. He had no name, but he was the right height and colouring, and that was enough.

Returning to the shore they mounted waiting horses and rode fast for Pompeii. With them was a small boy with black hair and features that were Poppy's.

33

POMPEII

Aeneus and Farzana awoke to an urgent knocking at their front door. They tumbled out of bed unsure what to expect.

'It's the middle of the night,' Aeneus complained. Farzana, stay where you are.'

'Who is it?' he shouted through the door.

'Praetorian Commander.'

As the door opened Tigellinus and Marcus entered looking tired and unkempt. They followed Aeneus to the kitchen.

'Please forgive our intrusion at this hour,' Tigellinus began, but Aeneus' eyes were intent on watching the boy with them.

'Farzana!' he called.

She entered the room then stood and stared. She had dark circles under her eyes and was obviously struggling to concentrate.

Gathering herself, she went to the boy, 'Rufrius?'

'Yes,' he whispered hesitantly.

Farzana gathered him into her arms and held him tightly She looked up at the two praetorians, her eyes full of tears. 'Please, tell me. How did Poppy die?'

Tigellinus left nothing out. If this woman would keep the boy safe then she and her husband deserved to know everything.

'May I suggest that you say the boy has come to you as the son of a dead relative?' Tigellinus said.

'This is a secret we must keep till the day we die,' Aeneus pledged solemnly as he took Farzana's hand. 'Everything we have we owe to Poppy. We will love her son.'

'And so will I!' they heard Aulus add from where he'd been standing unobserved at the back of the room.

'Gentlemen, can we get you some wine?' Aeneus offered.

'We must be going,' Tigellinus replied anxiously. 'As far as anyone knows, Rufrius died while out fishing. If Nero ever finds him, he'll be murdered and our lives will also be forfeit!' he cautioned.

'You're two brave men. It makes me proud to have once served as a praetorian,' Aeneus praised them as they left.

The three of them with the boy holding onto Farzana, stood speechless. They had no words.

Eventually, Farzana murmured softly, 'she knew she was going to die soon.'

'When did she tell you?' Aulus asked, puzzled.

'When I was staying with her at the villa.' I thought that she was just being overly emotional. But now I believe that somehow, she did know.'

That would become even more obvious as a few days passed. There were some unexpected events.

A couple of days later when Aeneus entered the Basilica to begin work, he was given a message to go to Clodius' office.

When he arrived, he found Clodius moodily staring out of the window.

'Salve, Aeneus. Come and sit just for a moment.'

Clodius went to a nearby chest and removed a package of documents which he handed to Aeneus. 'Our empress before she died left these with me. I gave an oath not to read them and I have not done so. I was told to give them to you if something ever happened to her. Perhaps, you'd like to take them to read in private in your office?'

Clutching the bundle, Clodius opened them one by one, wondering what new development awaited him. The first, was a letter in Poppy's own hand:

Farzana and Aeneus

There is an official document here that I hope you will never need to use. Keep it in a safe place. It will be much easier if no one realises that Rufrius is my son. I have written herewith, however, an acknowledgement of your right to him, in case something happens that I cannot foresee.

Please visit the House of the Vestals in Rome. My will is held there for safekeeping. The vestals will be expecting you. I have left everything to Farzana.

I am grateful for your love. I entrust my most precious son to you. I know you will keep his identity secret. May the gods bless you.

Poppy

The next read as follows:

Declared in Rome, 65 A.D.

In the event of my death I entrust my son, Rufrius, totally into the keeping of Farzana Capito and her husband, Aeneus Capito. This is my wish.

Note: My signature on this document has been officially witnessed.

Poppaea Augusta (Poppy)
Empress of Rome

Witness:

Tigellinus
Praetorian Commander

Rome
The Golden Palace

Tigellinus and Marcus returned to Rome after leaving Rufrius with Farzana and Aeneus hopefully, unobserved, but on high alert for any sign of danger. Until several days later, they thought that possibly Nero had forgotten the order he'd given.

'I haven't seen the boy,' he muttered irritably. 'Did you get rid of him?'

'I did,' Tigellinus replied, his severe expression unchanging. 'What did you do with him?'

'I had him drowned at sea. A fishing accident you could say.'

Nero waved his hand dismissively and turned away, the matter forgotten. It was never raised again.

34

House of the Vestals

Farzana stood at the entrance to the Vestals' House. There was no doubt that Poppy's death had caused utter turmoil for those she'd trusted. Slowly, Farzana approached the door and knocked. It was answered by a young vestal.

'How may I help you?

'I have been told to meet with you to claim a will left for safekeeping by a friend.

'Please follow me. So, you've lost someone dear to you?'

'She was like a sister to me,' Farzana answered softly.

'I'm so very sorry,' the vestal reached out to take her hand. 'I'll see if I can find it. What was her name?'

'Her name was Poppaea, but I knew her as Poppy. She was Empress of Rome.'

'Please wait.'

Only a few minutes later the vestal returned, this time with the senior vestal.

'Salve. What is your name?'

'My name is Farzana. This document of marriage will prove who I am.' She laid it before them.

'Then you are the rightful recipient of this will, Farzana. Would you like to sit in peace in one of our rooms beside the garden to read it?'

'I'd like that,' she accepted.

Farzana sat to read the will, a cup of watered wine having been provided to her.

When she'd finished reading, she sipped at the wine as she gazed out at the flowers, fragmented images of Poppy flitting through her mind. She'd come to the point where she was having difficulty processing all that had happened, beginning with her friend's death. Poppy had left her not only the magnificent villa at Oplontis but also enough gold to last them all far more than a lifetime.

The key to the villa was handed to her upon the officials accepting the authenticity of the will. She requested that the gold be held in a vault for that purpose in Rome. Only she had access.

It was time. The final scene would be played out.

Poppy's funeral had been arranged.

The day of Poppy's funeral was much the same as the day on which she'd been born, at least, as far as the weather that day. There were obvious differences, however, as there were bound to be even at the end of a life as short as hers.

Thousands of people gathered to line the route of the funeral procession from the Golden Palace to the Mausoleum of Augustus. It was distance enough to allow crowds to line the way without too much congestion. Most had come purely out of interest. Very few really knew very much about Poppy, but it was probably true that many blamed her, with good reason, for the death of Octavia.

Fascinated, Nero watched the people gathering, from a palace window. He had no intention of accepting blame for Poppy's untimely death. He'd spent a huge amount of money on costly eastern perfumes, incense and every conceivable item for her funeral. Unusually, Poppy was embalmed in the Egyptian fashion which caused considerable comment.

'Another performance begins,' Nero whispered to himself. 'This one will be my best.'

Nero had used the services of an expert in cosmetics to give his eyes the appearance of lengthy grief and weeping. His purple toga was perfect for the final touch. With solemn praetorians walking beside the casket and lining the roadway, the procession began the slow walk to Poppy's final resting place near the Tiber River.

Aeneus and Farzana stood watching in the crowd. When Nero appeared, weeping and utterly grief-stricken, she could hardly contain her anger.

'Goodbye, Poppy,' she whispered as her body was taken past them. She wished that her mother's burial place in Pompeii had been chosen for Poppy, but Nero had made a declaration that only the revered Mausoleum of Augustus was good enough for his precious empress.

A ripple of sadness went through some parts of the crowd as her body passed them. Others were simply silent.

Nero gave what he congratulated himself later was the performance of his life. When Poppy's final destination was reached, he had to be restrained as he wept copiously.

It could be said and was by some spectators later, that the whole funeral scene looked almost too much like a stage set.

All too soon it was over. Little by little, people turned away until the scene was bare except for a couple of praetorians still standing respectful guard in front of the tomb.

Daughter of Pompeii

'I've decided to marry that woman, Statilia Messalina,' Nero announced at a small dinner he held several days later. 'An emperor must have a wife,' he added with a laugh. The wedding was held not long after, as Nero prepared to make the long-planned trip to Greece. He found himself with a wife who was much quieter in nature than Poppy. Even though he'd executed her husband in order to marry Statilia, the marriage became less and less harmonious, however, she did accompany him to Greece.

'It's time to add more horses to my team!' Nero instructed Aelianus as he trained for the Greek Olympics which he'd had changed to the year of his visit. 'I must show them that I am a skilled charioteer.' He practised obsessively, day after day, until, finally, he departed for Greece with a huge retinue.

35

ROME

Nero had been away from Rome for far too long. It had been more than a few months, more like a year. If he expected to be met in Rome by cheering crowds rejoicing with him because of his exploits in Greece, he was to be sadly disappointed. No one seemed to even notice his arrival. Statilia sat beside him complaining, but he barely heard her. She was beginning to get on his nerves.

The recitals that had been added to the program in Greece purely for Nero's benefit, resulted not surprisingly, in a number of winning performances. How local competitors felt about that they kept to themselves. As for the main event, the chariot race, Nero had attempted far too much.

The Olympic chariot race had been a disaster. Unable to control his team of ten horses, Nero had fallen awkwardly out of the chariot when taking one of the turns and was fortunate not to have been killed. He did not cross the finishing line first.

He was, of course, declared the victor.

Nero had been urged to come back to Rome many times with warnings from Helius that the generals in the field were no longer loyal, and there was likely to be some sort of uprising, but he dallied in Greece far too long. It wasn't that he didn't believe the dispatches, but it was as if he somehow knew that what he had in this foreign land, was more fulfilling than anything else was ever likely to be again.

When he did return, he was obviously completely insane.

One of his final acts was to divorce Statilia. He could no longer stand the sight of her.

'You have command,' Tigellinus informed Marcus a few days later. 'As soon as the first of the generals reaches Rome they'll come for me. There is no way I can survive. I wish you well, they have no reason to arrest you.' He clapped Marcus on the shoulder. 'It's been an honour.'

'Travel well, my brother, perhaps the fates will be kind and I'll see you again. What reason should I give for your resignation?'

'Illness,' Tigellinus said without hesitation. 'The things I've had to do to please this emperor would make anyone ill.'

He travelled to his country house on the outskirts of the city, where he attempted to enjoy what he knew were his last days. He reflected on the one truly admirable thing he'd done, as he remembered a young boy with an innocent face and green eyes who'd called him 'Tigi.' It was enough.

Chaos broke out inside the palace a couple of days later, as the slaves began to desert their masters. Most took loot with them as they left. Nero waited, expecting calm to return, but it didn't. Urged to flee with the few praetorians and slaves still loyal to him he rode for Ostia.

'We have no ship for you,' every shipowner told him as he implored them to aid in his escape. 'You're a madman.' With revolts rising in the regions, Nero found himself with no support.

Returning to Rome he stayed in the palace overnight. He was deserted the following morning by the remaining praetorians, many of whom despised him. With the senate meeting in an attempt to find a negotiated way out of the chaos especially as there was no heir, Nero fled the city with four remaining freedmen. In the curia the senators argued over the best course of action. If they moved against Nero who would take the throne?

And Galba came closer and closer to Rome.

'I have a villa not far out of the city,' Phaon shouted as they ran, 'we may be safe there.'

'I just need a place of peace for a time. I can't believe it. Not even a gladiator would come forward to kill me when I asked for help,' Nero whined.

Disguised, they ran from Rome and down the country road that led to the villa. No one seemed to recognise them and no one stopped them to ask who they were. Once there they lay down to rest.

'Epaphroditos, you and the others must dig me a grave,' Nero insisted. 'I must have a grave.'

Neophytos stood and taking up a shovel began to dig the earth. 'I'll dig it,' he offered, defeated.

Nero sat down outside the door, his mind racing. There was no way out. This was all the wrong way around. It wasn't supposed to end this way. Emperors killed people, not the reverse. Returning inside he found a shallow grave waiting for him.

'I can't do it. Not by myself!' Nero exclaimed. He looked nervously around the group who all looked away, unable to meet his gaze.

'Epaphroditos, you must be the one.' Nero held the gladius and gestured him to come forward. As he still held back, Nero attempted to kill himself but only partially succeeded, at which time Epaphroditos finished the task.

Galba's men rode up as they stood looking at Nero's corpse. They found to their satisfaction that he was, indeed, dead.

Nero's body was thrown into a nearby ditch and left to rot.

News of the Emperor's death quickly spread to the senate. They immediately declared him, posthumously, to be "an enemy of the people of Rome."

They were eager to please Galba.

Tigellinus sat in his villa in his favourite chair dressed in his uniform, as he watched through the window for the signal he knew he would eventually see. He'd taken an oath to protect the Emperor and he'd done his duty. He genuinely believed that no one could have done better. He had few regrets. His gladius lay on the table beside him.

He dozed off for a while and when he awoke it wasn't long before he saw, in the distance, a cloud of dust rising from the road as Galba's men approached on horseback.

Calmly, Tigellinus picked up his gladius and killed himself.

Antium

(South of Rome)

68 A.D.

Acte stood alone, motionless, on the edge of the clifftop as the waves from a raging sea smashed against the man-made caves below, and the cold wind tugged and pulled at her sending her dark hair flying. She was soaked to the skin but seemed unaware.

Just one more step and it could all be over.

Suddenly, Acte shook herself free from her reverie and decided to turn back towards the large palace behind her, the place of Nero's birth. Only a few servants remained to provide for her needs. The gods knew as well as she did, that she needed little, and would soon return to Velitrae where she'd made her home for many years.

There was only one last service she could provide for the man she'd loved more than any other in this world. But, to do it, she must return to the cesspit of Rome, to the scheming, corrupt senators and the fickle rabble. She would bury Nero.

On reaching Rome, Acte hired several strong men to assist her. Rumours seemed to indicate that Nero had been killed at the farmhouse of the freedman, Phaon, just outside the city. She decided to begin there.

It didn't take long for them to find Nero's corpse lying in a ditch by the farmhouse door. The odour and appearance of the body almost caused those lifting it to puke.

'This wasn't what I expected,' one of the men complained, 'it's putrid.'

'We'll need more money,' another demanded and they all nodded.

'I'll pay all of you double my first offer,' Acte offered to be sure they'd finish the job.

The body was lavished with perfumed oils and unguents and placed on a pyre. In all, Acte paid 300,000 sestercii to provide the funeral. Finally, it was done and Nero's remains burned on a flaming pyre. A few passers-by gathered on the Pincian Hill at the tomb of the Ahenobarbi to watch, most of them unaware of the identity of the body. Ironically, Nero died on the sixth anniversary of Octavia's execution.

Acte returned to Velitrae where she is said to have had a quiet life. Thanks to Nero, she lived in great comfort, able to purchase whatever she desired, finding comfort in the arms of one of her slaves who'd been with her for many years.

Locusta's Country Estate

Locusta no longer worried as she would have done once about retribution for her actions. It seemed that with the exception of those wanting to learn her skills, the world had forgotten her.

She was comfortable and had sufficient funds to pay for anything she needed. She'd worked hard and taken risks to afford what she had now.

The old fear was back, though, when she heard Nero had committed suicide. She'd taken to glancing fearfully out of the front window now and again.

One day all of her fears were realised. Praetorians were seen advancing on the house. She knew any attempt at escape would be hopeless. There was nowhere to run. She stood waiting for them, her head held high, as some of her students looked on curiously.

'Your name is Locusta?'

'Yes.'

'You are under arrest for murder.'

'Whose murder?'

'There are many.'

Locusta's heart sank. This time it was deadly serious and there was no one to protect her.

They bound her hands and forced her to walk with them back to the city. She was once again imprisoned in the Tullianum prison.

'Well, well!' The same guard was still there doing the same job. 'It's been a while, Locusta. How are you going to get out this time?'

Locusta spat at him. She crawled away into a corner and from that moment said not one word to anyone. A couple of days later she was dragged out again into the light, attempting to shield her eyes from the sun's brightness.

There she was paraded through the streets and heckled by the crowd. It was later recorded that those carrying out the execution had been ordered to make an example of her.

Only those there that day know how.

The Villa at Oplontis

The years that followed were a joy for Farzana and Aeneus. Surprisingly, they had no children of their own but their love for Rufrius was total.

'What do you want to be when you grow up?' Aeneus asked him one day as they were all playing in the garden.

'I want to be a soldier like you were, Dad,' he answered. He hesitated and then added, 'and like Tigi.'

In the years since the deaths of Tigellinus and Nero, they'd never been mentioned in front of Rufrius.

'What do you remember about Tigi?' Farzana asked curiously.

'He was big and strong and I liked him.'

'I'm glad,' she answered. 'He was a good man.'

Several years after they'd moved to Oplontis, Aulus died. Although they were prepared in the sense that he was at an age where that was always likely, it still had a serious impact on the family. Farzana would occasionally forget and turn to speak to him as if he was still with them, before remembering sadly that he was gone.

She liked to sit on the bench under the plane tree remembering her time with Poppy. She watched events in Rome purely because of Rufrius, but with the eventual rise of

Daughter of Pompeii

Vespasian to Emperor she ceased to be quite as concerned. He was a different kind of emperor. He came from peasant stock and had few delusions of grandeur.

One day, when Rufrius was old enough to understand, she'd tell him who he really was and most of all, who his mother was and what she'd been like. She'd also tell him about Tigellinus, who'd saved his life.

This was necessary so that he'd know his place in the world, and if anyone ever found out his true identity he could take precautions for his safety. Rufrius would always be a potential threat to anyone seeking to take the throne.

What Farzana did not know, was that their story was not yet quite finished.

Part IV

79 A.D.

At the End

36

POMPEII

September 79 A.D.

Caecilius Jucundus frowned with displeasure as he stared at the elaborate central fountain in his back garden. 'Still no water,' he muttered irritably under his breath. He was becoming an old man. He glanced up at a sky the colour of gunmetal, shaking his head in annoyance. It occurred to him that it was eerily quiet, but there was nothing else of any note to be seen or heard, except, perhaps, for wisps of what looked like steam coming from the top of the mountain that loomed over the city. He returned inside to ready himself for a meeting that morning with a vineyard owner who was seeking funds to set up his own export business.

Not far away, in Via di Castricio, Livia and Drusilla were enjoying their usual morning gossip as they sat in the perfume shop. Both of their businesses were doing well and the women with quite content with their lives.

'I wish they'd fix the water, though!' Livia complained.

'It's not so bad for me,' Drusilla laughed. My perfume sales are so high I'll be running out of some scents soon. If there's not enough water to bathe, people have to use something haven't they!'

On the other side of the city, in the scribe's shop, Vibius had struggled out of bed and was considering what was in the house to eat. He'd had a good sleep last night after taking some of his poppy potion and was feeling positive about the day ahead. He was expecting more work to come in shortly from one of his regular customers, and for once, his fingers weren't aching. He sat idly for a while watching a variety of people passing in front of his house and up the laneway. There was always something happening in Pompeii. Soon, he fell asleep.

Not far from him, Lucius Diomedes sat in his villa writing an appeal to the senate in Rome, requesting additional money to allow repairs to be continued in the city. The money so far allocated had all but run out. There was still much to be done and it seemed to be taking forever to complete. Lucius had already contributed from his own personal funds but even he couldn't keep doing that. Alerted before long to the escalating activity of Vesuviius, Lucius fled the city with Julia Felix.

Close to the Nola Gate, Varus was still asleep in his room at the inn after a night's drinking. It was unlikely that he'd wake up before lunch and when he did, he would have a monster of a headache. He mumbled in his sleep, twisting and turning. There was no one there to care. He later died in the colonnade of the Palaestra as he tried to flee through the nearby city gate.

At the gladiator barracks, next to the theatre, preparations were well underway for the afternoon's performance. The lanister watched as the men warmed up using wooden posts and swords. Apart from an occasional word here or there he seemed satisfied with preparations. After lunch in the barracks, they lined up to make their way to the great amphitheatre.

Aeneus frowned as he left the Basilica to make his way to the Inn of Euxinus for lunch. Something didn't feel quite right, and he shuddered. Glancing up at the sky, his alarm grew as he saw threatening-looking steam rising up from Vesuvius. It was no better when he'd finished lunch. In fact, it seemed to be worse. He put his hand up to his forehead as grey flakes of ash began to fall.

Farzana and Rufrius were both at home at the villa so at least he knew where they were. Calling a messenger, he despatched word to them to stay there until he reached them. Within a short time he'd cleared his desk, then he immediately left the Basilica to return to the villa.

It wasn't long before the volume of ash increased, putting a stop to the gladiator games and causing alarm amongst the people, who fled from the amphitheatre in panic. Many ran to their homes and took shelter.

Around noon, a column of pumice exploded from the volcano. It extended in an umbrella-like cloud above Vesuvius, as high in the sky as anyone could see. Soon, large pieces of rocks fell, causing injury to some of those gathering in the streets especially in the forum and other public spaces.

Then came the darkness.

Slaves, shackled to the bars of their cells lining the perimeter of the macellum began to scream for help, but in the chaos, their cries went unheard.

Overloaded with pumice, the roofs of many villas crashed inwards, falling to the ground with a thunderous roar. The noise level in the city increased, and many grabbed whatever possessions they could carry either on their person or in carts and began to leave through the city gates which were soon congested.

Early on the morning of the second day, the huge funnel above Vesuvius fell in on itself and there were two pyroclastic surges from the volcano that did not reach Pompeii. The third, soon after, reached Pompeii's Herculaneum Gate. The fourth, an hour and a half later, entered the city and was followed by two more surges that overwhelmed it, burying it and killing anyone who'd remained, including the slaves in the macellum.

Farzana, Aeneus and Rufrius did not die in the eruption. Aeneus' quick thinking led them to abandon the villa at Oplontis and flee with their wealth to Napoli, where they found safety. Poppy's magnificent villa was badly damaged but not totally destroyed.

Others, aged or ill like the scribe, Vibius, would no doubt have remained and been killed, or tried to flee but been overcome by the effort. Some did find safety, but the terror they'd witnessed would have remained with them for the rest of their lives.

Epilogue

POMPEII

Archaeological excavations
Via Consolare

2017

The heat was already beginning to rise on another blazing hot summer's day in Pompeii. There was no cover from the sun in this grey city, its buildings roofless, its people gone.

Most of all, there was no colour.

Sandro scanned the city as far as he could see as he stood on a slight rise opposite the suburban baths. He closed his eyes then slowly opened them again. People milled around at the top of Marine Parade some heading for the forum, others were walking towards the temple of Isis or further on to the amphitheatre. Some made their way up Via Stabiana on their way to Via Consolare or the Villa of the Mysteries, just outside the city walls.

But they were not the people of today.

Life in front of him teemed with colour.

Sandro had long possessed the gift of being able to imagine what a city would have been like, where life took him back nearly two thousand years. That was why he'd been determined to work as an archaeologist specialising in restoration.

He'd been waiting for a long time before he gained a place with a team working in Pompeii. There was always a shortage of money, made worse by the very size of the excavated city, which surprised most visitors.

It was finally possible for restoration teams to excavate, and even restore, now sufficient funds were available to return Pompeii's exquisite frescoes to their former magnificence. Members of his team, tired after a long day, were involved in work requiring both skill and patience. They had the pleasure with each finished fresco of seeing the difference restoration made to the brilliance of the colours and the freshness, as if each had only been painted yesterday.

They were restoring wall frescoes amongst the most beautiful to be seen in the whole of Pompeii. That was surprising, given the section of the city in which they were excavating and the ruins of this house, which indicated a small, inexpensive dwelling similar to those structures around it.

At first, Sandro thought he was imagining things. He peered more closely at the fresco he was restoring. But what he was looking at didn't seem to make sense.

'I think I may have found something interesting,' he called to his supervisor as he rose from where he'd been kneeling. Sandro pointed to the bottom of the fresco at the very right-hand side of the painting and down towards the bottom.

'The damaged paint came off more easily in this patch than in the remainder of the work,' he explained.

'Bring me a magnifying glass!' Marco, the supervisor, requested as he hurried over and knelt to examine it.

Sandro held his breath as Marco studied the tiny patch.

'It appears we have somewhat of a mystery here. I don't know what it means, maybe someone else will,' he finally declared, shaking his head. 'Make sure it's photographed before anything more is done with it.' He walked away leaving Sandro to stare at it, perplexed.

Beneath the red roses originally painted by the artist was tiny writing. It was an enigmatic message and the team members shook their heads, defeated as to its meaning.

Farzana
My son is your son
Poppy

OTHER NOVELS BY THIS AUTHOR

POMPEII: DEATH COMES CALLING
WHISPERS FROM POMPEII

CLEOPATRA: WHISPERS FROM THE NILE

MEDICI: THE QUEEN'S PERFUME
THE TITUS CONSPIRACY
ARSINOE OF EPHESUS (Novella)

WITH THANKS

Professor Miles Prince

Dr. Harold Cashmore

ACKNOWLEDGEMENT

Front cover design by London Montgomery

HISTORICAL NOTES

It's been an interesting journey researching the woman history knows as Poppaea Sabina, Empress of Rome. To avoid confusion, as her mother had the same name, she is known in this novel as Poppy.

The writings of ancient historians have information about certain events in her life, but it is limited. The picture they present is one of a beautiful, ambitious and ruthless woman. That these writers at that time had a point of view biased against her is probable.

To find the truth it is necessary not only to look at the overall picture of the time in which she lived, but most of all, her personal circumstances and reasons for many of her actions.

Occasionally, to enhance the flow of the novel, it has been necessary to alter timelines of some events and to fill in the details of what might have taken place. I have remained true to the historical facts as much as possible.

Some events are known which certainly could be expected to have affected Poppy's behaviour and attitudes. Her family circumstances are as described and the suicide of her mother, an innocent victim, due to the malevolence of the Empress, Messalina, is referred to by historians.

Farzana and her family are fictional characters. The young Poppy probably did have a close friend but we do not know. She was born in Pompeii and belonged to a wealthy, minor patrician family.

It is impossible to consider Poppy without placing her in context as a wife to Nero. His behaviour degenerated as years went by in his reign, until he is acknowledged to have been insane at the time of his death.

Important supporting historical players in the drama of Poppy's life are those such as Acte, Locusta and Tigellinus. The basic facts are as I have described them but with some minor, fictional enhancement.

The Villa of Oplontis must have been magnificent. A wedding present to Poppy from Nero, the ruins stand just outside Pompeii and can still be visited today. It is a shadow of its former glory, but enough can be seen to appreciate how stunning it must have been. The huge swimming pool has long been empty, but remains as a monument to those who constructed it so long ago.

Archaeological finds have enabled us to be reasonably sure of the location in which Poppy would have lived in Pompeii before her marriage. They were a family with a background in tile manufacturing, from which they made the money to build the villa described in the novel.

Nero's Domus Aurea (House of Gold) is difficult for us to picture in its enormity and extravagance. Nero brought the economy of Rome to near destruction as he poured every possible resource into the building of his dream. After his death other buildings were built over the top of it and Vespasian replaced the pleasure palace with the killing theatre of death, the Flavian Amphitheatre. (The Colosseum.)

In this novel, the role of the praetorian guards has been highlighted. They are the forgotten power group in Rome, who could place an emperor on his throne or just as quickly tear him down. There were praetorians in barracks in Nuceria and Naples and certainly on patrols in Pompeii.

There are interesting disagreements historically, in terms of certain events in the time period this story covers. These are as follows:

The Great Fire of Rome
Who started the worst fire in Rome's history?
It was probably not Nero. He is known to have been away in Antium at the time and to have returned to the city to give assistance. Besides, why would he burn part of his own palace? Did he take the opportunity afterwards to build his new Golden Palace on former public land? The simple answer is *yes*.

Was it Tigellinus?
This is thought to have been unlikely. It is true that there was a group of men seen throwing blazing torches into the fire to restart it when it looked like dying out. There is no historical proof as to who these men were.

Was it the Christians?
We need to consider what the Christians were like at this time. They were a small cult made up primarily of the poor and slaves. Their belief was one of peace.

Was it the Jews?
The finger of suspicion must rest with them.
Only the Jewish area of the city was left untouched by the fire. Their attitude to Rome was volatile and only two years later

they revolted in Judea. Poppy's part, if any, in this situation is of interest. Historians consider that she, and her mother, were Jewish. Archaeologists have not yet found a synagogue in Pompeii but it is likely that there was at least a small one. Historically, Poppy is known to have had meetings alone at the palace with Jewish leaders. It's possible that she sought to protect them.

Did Nero Murder Poppy?

Historians tell us that Nero returned to the palace on the day of the murder after having been to the Circus Maximus. At this time in his reign he could certainly be considered as being already mentally unstable.

We are also told that there was some kind of an argument between the two. History does not record the reason, except a supposition that he might have been late returning from the chariot races. The question has to be asked, would that have been enough to cause such a violent argument? It is unlikely. Was Poppy's death an accident or murder?

It is necessary to look at Nero's behaviour after her death in order to have any possibility of finding the answer. The known facts are interesting.

First, as described in the novel, Poppy did have a son to her first husband, named Rufrius, after his father. Historians tell us that not long after Poppy's death, Nero ordered him to be murdered in a "fishing accident." This is more likely to have been the action of an extremely guilty man who perhaps hated his wife. Otherwise, one would have expected Nero to have gone the other way and showered the boy with love, in memory of his beloved mother.

Second, Nero married very quickly after Poppy's death to a woman named Statilia. She is reported to have been of loose morals, although beautiful.

In my opinion, Nero did murder Poppy in a rage. Perhaps she fell first, but whatever the case, he repeatedly kicked her. She was heavily pregnant.

Poppy's Funeral
The absolute excesses of Poppy's funeral could well be seen as suspicious. Standing watching from afar, the whole 'performance' looks really excessive, even for an empress. Reading available historical documents, it seems that the scene was very much like a stage setting with Nero as the main mourner. Perhaps he was that and more. He considered himself a great actor. He would also have chosen to come out of the whole thing appearing innocent and distraught. This may have been the ultimate performance of his life.

Other Characters & Places

The name of Aeneus Capito of the X cohort of the praetorians from Nuceria comes from an ancient graffito scratched on a Pompeii wall.

Prima's real name was Primigenia. There are many references to her on the walls of public buildings in Pompeii and Herculaneum such as a bathhouse. She was a beautiful, elite courtesan.

Greetings to Primigenia...I would wish to become a signet ring for no more than an hour so that I might give you kisses....

Grafitto

Locusta was a notorious poisoner. There is a record of her execution but without reliable details of the manner in which it was carried out.

Acte, mistress to Nero early in his reign, appears to have remained loyal to him. Historical accounts describe how she buried him at considerable cost in the company of two of his old nurses after he'd been left unburied in a ditch.

Tigellinus. There are conflicting historical accounts about this Prefect of the Praetorians. I have written his character as I believe he might have been.

Portus

Satellite archaeology has identified a large, previously unknown amphitheatre lying between Ostia and Portus. The latter was the site of a huge port complex developed by Claudius, which now lies under Fiumicino Airport.

The Calpurnius Piso Conspiracy

In 65 A.D. A group of up to thirty conspirators planned to assassinate Nero. These included the other Praetorian Prefect, Fanius Rufus and the satirist, Petronius. They were unsuccessful.

In conclusion, I see Poppy as a complex personality. It is sometimes said that one must go back to the early life of a person to seek answers as to their future actions.

As a young woman of fourteen years old at the time, one can only imagine the burning hatred and wish for revenge that would have formed Poppy's thinking, after the shocking 'forced' suicide of her mother. That she became ruthlessly ambitious is highly probable, in her quest to bring down and control the system that had destroyed her.

Poppy had no family left of her own except her small son, Rufrius. She must have known towards the end, as Nero's sanity degenerated, that she was in danger. It is reasonable to expect that she'd have made whatever arrangements she found possible and most advantageous for her son, should she not survive.

I have given Poppy the friends she would have needed to anchor her during her reign as the most powerful and wealthy woman in the Roman Empire. That she was as loyal and generous to them as described is quite possible and helps to balance her less admirable traits. Her actions towards Octavia cannot be justified. It is necessary to bear in mind, however, the tolerated practices of the day, especially amongst the elite and the environment in which they lived.

ANCIENT POMPEII

1. Villa of the Mysteries
2. Villa of Diomedes
3. Herculaneum Gate
4. Suburban Bathhouse
5. Forum
6. Large theatre
7. Small theatre
8. Amphitheatre
9. Harbour
10. Temple of Venus
11. Via delle Tombe
12. Via Consolare
13. Via del Vesuvio
14. Via di Nola
15. Vicolo del Centenario
16. Via Stabiana
17. Via Marina
18. Via dell' Abbondanza
19. Via dei Teatri
20. Via di Castricio
21. Via di Nocera

The Author

Lorraine Blundell (Parsons) was born in Brisbane, Australia. She lives in Melbourne and has a daughter, Jenni, and a son, Steve. Lorraine Graduated from the University of Queensland with a Bachelor of Arts Degree majoring in English and History. She holds a teaching qualification in Drama from Trinity College, London.

She trained as a classical singer at the Queensland State Conservatorium of Music, Brisbane. Spanning that period she sang professionally on television as a solo vocalist, regularly performing on channels BTQ7 and QTQ9 Brisbane as well as nationally on HSV7 Melbourne.

Lorraine is an experienced performer in amateur musical theatre productions. Her interests are singing, ancient history and archaeology.

Printed in Great Britain
by Amazon